She felt his eyes o

He watched her every move as she came downstairs from putting the kids to bed.

"Thanks for babysitting," she said. "And for the pizza. I'm sure you have more exciting plans for your Friday night, but I appreciate that you stayed."

"I didn't have plans. And I enjoyed hanging out with you and the kids."

She sat across from him. "You're my daughter's new BFF, you know."

His eyes glinted. "We're more than BFFs. She asked me to marry her."

"Well, you gave her flowers and played Barbies with her. Of course she's head over heels in love with you."

"Is that all it takes?"

"For a three-year-old."

He leaned forward and settled his hands on her knees. Even through the denim she felt the heat of his touch—a heat that seared her whole body. "What about the three-year-old's mom?"

She eyed him warily. "Are you flirting with me?"

"If you have to ask, my skills must be rusty."

"It's more likely that mine are," she admitted, feeling out of her element here.

He lowered his head toward her. "Then maybe we should work on changing that."

THOSE ENGAGING GARRETTS!
—The Carolina Cousins

Dear Reader,

I have to admit, I'm not a fan of most reality-TV programs. But I have always enjoyed watching home-improvement shows, especially seeing the "before" and "after" of a room makeover—and especially if the show includes a good-looking guy in a tool belt.

That's how the idea for *Ryder to the Rescue* came to be. The first mention of this homegrown show on Charisma's WNCC-TV was in *A Forever Kind of Family* and, as many of the female residents of this town were falling in love with the handsome handyman, I was happy to discover that my readers were, too.

However, the seeds for this story were sown even earlier, when readers were introduced to Lauryn Garrett in *The Daddy Wish*. Back then, Lauryn was a young expectant mother living with her husband in a fixer-upper. Now she's a divorced mother with two young kids living under the leaky roof of a never-been-fixed fixer-upper.

It's a match made in television-ratings heaven!

But as eager as Ryder is to get his hands on Lauryn's house, it is the wounded woman and her adorable children who grab hold of his heart. And as he concentrates his efforts on renovating their home, the kids are focused on a different project: building the perfect daddy! And he's beginning to look a lot like Ryder Wallace...

I hope you enjoy their story!

Happy Reading,

Brenda Harlen

Building the Perfect Daddy

Brenda Harlen

HARLEQUIN®SPECIAL EDITION®

Recycling programs
for this product may
not exist in your area.

ISBN-13: 978-0-373-65988-3

Building the Perfect Daddy

Copyright © 2016 by Brenda Harlen

HARLEQUIN®
www.Harlequin.com

Printed in U.S.A.

Brenda Harlen is a former attorney who once had the privilege of appearing before the Supreme Court of Canada. The practice of law taught her a lot about the world and reinforced her determination to become a writer—because in fiction, she could promise a happy ending! Now she is an award-winning, national bestselling author of more than thirty titles for Harlequin. You can keep up-to-date with Brenda on Facebook and Twitter or through her website, brendaharlen.com.

Books by Brenda Harlen

Harlequin Special Edition

Those Engaging Garretts!

Two Doctors & a Baby
The Bachelor Takes a Bride
A Forever Kind of Family
The Daddy Wish
A Wife for One Year
The Single Dad's Second Chance
A Very Special Delivery
His Long-Lost Family
From Neighbors...to Newlyweds?

Montana Mavericks: What Happened at the Wedding?

Merry Christmas, Baby Maverick!

Montana Mavericks: 20 Years in the Saddle!

The Maverick's Thanksgiving Baby

Montana Mavericks: Rust Creek Cowboys

A Maverick under the Mistletoe

Montana Mavericks: Back in the Saddle

The Maverick's Ready-Made Family

Visit the Author Profile page
at Harlequin.com for more titles.

This book is dedicated to my wonderful husband,
who has proved, time and again over the years,
he is capable of tackling the various
home improvements our various homes
have required (with thanks for finally putting up
the new trim in the hallway!).

Chapter One

It was raining again.

The sound of the water drumming on the roof woke Lauryn up well before her seven-month-old son. She cracked an eyelid and squinted at the glowing numbers of her alarm clock—5:28 a.m.

Way too freakin' early.

She rolled over and pulled the covers up over her head, as if that might muffle the ominous sound of the rain. When she'd had a couple of leaky spots patched in the spring, the roofer had warned her that the whole thing needed to be redone. She'd nodded her understanding because she did understand. Unfortunately, she didn't have the money for that kind of major expense right now, and the sound of the water pounding down felt like Mother Nature beating on her head, chastising her for the foolish choices she'd made.

But she was no longer the idealistic twenty-seven-year-old who had been as much in love with the idea of being a bride as the man who had proposed to her. And she was still paying for that mistake—which was why she couldn't afford a new roof right now.

She looked up at the ceiling and sent up a silent prayer: *Please hold out for just one more year. Just long enough for me figure out my finances and my life.*

She didn't know who she was trying to bargain with— the roof or Mother Nature or God. At this point, she would willingly make a deal with anyone who had the power to change her fate.

Her parents—Tom and Susan Garrett—had given her and Rob the money to buy a house when they'd married. A proper house, like the simple Craftsman-style bungalow in Ridgemount that she'd thought would be perfect for a young couple starting out. But she'd let her charming new husband convince her that they could split the money between a less expensive fixer-upper and his start-up sporting-goods business, The Locker Room.

After six years, the house was still in need of major repairs, the business was failing and she was on her own with a preschooler and a baby. Was it any wonder that she only wanted to stay in bed all day with the covers over her head?

But she didn't have that option. She didn't get to follow her bliss, as Rob had claimed he was doing when he walked away from all of his responsibilities. She was stuck right where she was with the old roof, drafty windows, leaky plumbing and rotting porch.

Still, she tried to focus on the positive—her final divorce papers had come in the mail a few days earlier and she was grateful that it was done. She might have wished away her entire marriage, except then she wouldn't have Kylie and Zachary.

No matter what happened, she was determined not to let her mistakes impact their lives. She had to figure a way out of the precarious situation they were in, to give them a stable and loving home. Hopefully, the way out would be found within the business plan she'd prepared for her upcoming meeting at the bank, because taking more money from her family was definitely *not* an option.

She glanced at the clock again—5:57 a.m.

Knowing that Zachary would be up within the hour, she reluctantly pushed back the covers and slid out of bed. Avoiding the creakier floorboards, she tiptoed to his room to confirm that he was sleeping soundly in his crib. He was so big already. Almost eighteen pounds and twenty-eight inches long at his last checkup, he'd long since mastered rolling from his back to his stomach and over again and was now starting to use the rails of his crib to pull himself up.

She gently touched the ends of his baby-soft curls and felt her heart swell inside of her chest. She might hate her ex-husband for a lot of reasons, but she would always be grateful to him for the two precious children he'd given her.

Moving away from the crib, she headed to the master bath. Stripping away the tank top and boxer shorts she'd slept in, she showered quickly, determined to have herself put together and ready for the day before either of the kids woke up. But she hadn't even finished drying her hair when she heard the baby stirring. Zachary was inevitably up with the sun, but apparently he knew seven in the morning even when the sun wasn't shining.

She hurried downstairs to fix him a bottle of formula. He was eating some solid foods now and drinking from a sippy cup during the day, but a bottle continued to be part of his early morning and late-night routine, and Lauryn appreciated the quiet time snuggling with her baby. She returned to the bedroom with the bottle in hand and lifted him from his crib, changed his diaper and settled into the rocking chair by the window to feed him.

When Zachary was satisfied—at least for the moment— she headed across the hall to check on her daughter. Stepping into the little girl's bedroom was like stepping into the pages of a fairy tale. The interior walls were painted to look like they were made of stone blocks, with three arched "windows" providing spectacular views of the kingdom, including snowcapped mountains, a lush green forest and even a waterfall spilling into a crystal-clear lake. There was also an exquisite glass carriage drawn by a pair of white horses making its way down a long, winding road toward another castle with numerous turrets and towers. The castle was guarded by knights and dragons; there were wildflowers in the grass, fairies peeking out from the trees and butterflies, birds and hot air balloons in the sky.

She didn't know how many hours her sister had spent, first sketching and then painting the mural. Jordyn had created a complete fantasy world for her niece, and Kylie absolutely loved everything about it. It was only Lauryn who had recently started to worry that she wasn't doing her little girl any favors by encouraging her belief in fairy tales and happily-ever-afters.

Lauryn used to believe in those same things. And when Rob Schulte had proposed, she'd been certain that he was her Prince Charming. Even during the rocky periods in their marriage, she'd been confident that their love would guide them through the difficult terrain. And she'd remained optimistic right up until the day her prince had ridden off into the sunset with a yoga instructor, leaving her trapped in a crumbling castle surrounded by fire-breathing dragons in the form of unpaid creditors.

It had taken her a while, but she'd eventually come to accept that he'd never loved her the way she'd loved him. She could forgive him for walking out on their marriage—but not for walking away from their children. She was relieved, but not really surprised, that Rob hadn't shown any inclination to fight for custody. She had enough struggles trying to manage the business he'd left floundering and keep a leaky roof over all of their heads without battling on yet another front.

As she made her way down to the kitchen, Zachary let out a loud belch, then a relieved sigh.

She continued to rub his back as he settled. "Does that feel better now?"

The baby, of course, didn't answer.

Feeling dampness on her shoulder, she tore a paper towel off the roll and attempted to wipe off the spit-up that was now sliding down the front of her shirt. Obviously she would have to change, but Kylie would be up soon and she wanted to get her breakfast started.

She settled Zachary in his high chair with a handful of Cheerios on his tray to keep him occupied while she gathered the necessary ingredients to make French toast. Hopefully Kylie's favorite breakfast would make the little girl more amenable to spending the afternoon with her grandparents while Lauryn attended her meeting at the bank.

Susan and Tom Garrett absolutely doted on their grandchildren, and Kylie had always loved spending time with them, but since Rob had gone, the little girl had become unusually clingy and demanding. It was as if she was afraid to let her mother out of her sight in case she disappeared from her life, too.

Lauryn was turning the first slice of bread in the pan when she heard Kylie's footsteps on the stairs. A moment later, her daughter trudged into the kitchen, wearing her favorite princess nightgown made of a silky pink fabric with a ruffled hem, white silk underskirt and puffy sleeves—and a decidedly *un*-princess-like scowl on her face. Kylie had never been a morning person.

Climbing into her booster seat at the table, she reached for the cup of orange juice waiting for her. Lauryn cut up the fried bread and set the plate in front of her daughter, who picked up her fork and stabbed a piece of toast. Lauryn sat beside her and sipped her coffee.

Kylie finished about half of her breakfast, then pushed her plate aside. "Can we go to the park today?"

"Maybe later," Lauryn said.

"I wanna go now," her daughter insisted.

"It's raining now," she said. "And Mama has to take care of some paperwork this morning."

Kylie folded her arms over her chest in an all-too-familiar mutinous posture. "I wanna go to the park."

"Later," she promised, kissing the top of her daughter's

head before lifting Zachary out of his high chair. "Right now, we have to get the two of you washed up and dressed."

She'd just propped the baby on her hip when the doorbell rang. Kylie immediately raced down the hall.

With a weary sigh, Lauryn followed. If it had been up to her, she would have ignored the summons. She wasn't in the mood to deal with some kid selling chocolate bars or magazine subscriptions, especially when she could afford neither. And why anyone would be going door-to-door on a Wednesday morning in this weather was beyond her comprehension, but since Kylie had already climbed up on the sofa in the living room and was pushing the curtains apart to see who was at the door, she could hardly pretend that no one was home.

"There's lotsa peoples outside," Kylie told her.

Lots of people?

Lauryn knew she was frowning when she unlocked the door and pulled it open—a frown that deepened when she saw that her daughter hadn't been exaggerating. In addition to the mouthwateringly handsome and impressively muscled man on her porch wearing a hard hat and a tool belt—*Oh, please God, do* not *let this be some kind of stripper-gram, because I have no idea how I'd explain* that *to my daughter*— there was a man on the lawn with what looked like a video camera propped on his shoulder, a trio of people standing a little farther away under an umbrella and a van and two pickup trucks parked on the road in front of the house.

The hunk in the hard hat and the tool belt smiled, causing a fluttery sensation in her belly, along with a nagging suspicion that she'd seen him somewhere before.

"Are you Lauryn Schulte?" he asked.

"I am," she confirmed, her tone giving no hint of the unexpected and unwelcome awareness she was feeling. "But unless you're from the North Carolina State Lottery with one of those big checks for me, you can get yourself and your camera crew off my property."

Chapter Two

The experiences gained from three years in front of the camera had taught Ryder Wallace to keep a smile on his face under almost any circumstances. Circumstances certainly more challenging than a frazzled mother with a baby on her hip and what looked like baby vomit on the shoulder of the pale yellow T-shirt she wore over faded denim jeans.

Except that she then closed the door in his smiling face. *And locked it.*

He actually heard the click of the dead bolt sliding into place.

Not quite the reaction he'd anticipated.

"Cut!"

Owen Diercks jogged over to the rickety porch, where Ryder was still staring, slack jawed, at the closed door.

"What in the hell just happened?" the director demanded.

"I think we came at a bad time," Ryder said.

"I'm tired of standing around waiting for these women to primp for the camera," Owen grumbled. "Whoever decided to surprise the contest winners obviously didn't think that one through."

"I believe the surprise aspect was your idea," Ryder said, although the home owner's tone made him suspect that Lauryn Schulte's reasons for closing the door on his face were about more than an unwillingness to face the cameras without her lipstick on.

"Which is probably why no one ever listens to my ideas,"

the director acknowledged as lightning flashed in the distance. He glanced at the sky, a worried look on his face, then at his watch. "I don't particularly want to stand around in the rain for God only knows how long while our home owner does her hair and makeup."

"Do you want to wrap for today?" Ryder asked him.

"No, I want to stay on schedule," Owen grumbled as thunder rumbled and lightning flashed again. "But it doesn't look like that's going to happen today."

Ryder glanced back at Carl, who was using a garbage bag to keep his camera sheltered from the rain while he waited for further instructions.

"Pack it up," Owen called out to him.

Carl nodded and immediately moved toward the van with his equipment. The assistant to the director and the AV tech followed the cameraman.

"We need to get back on schedule," Owen said. "Which means that someone needs to remind Mrs. Schulte of the terms and conditions she agreed to when she submitted her application." He looked at Ryder. "Do you want me to do it?"

"I will," he offered. Because as great as Owen was in handling the numerous and various aspects of his job, he also had a tendency to piss people off. And after only a brief interaction with Lauryn Schulte, Ryder got the impression that she was already pissed off.

Owen nodded. "I expect to be back here first thing Monday morning with everyone ready to go."

"They will be," Ryder promised, with more conviction than he felt.

As the director made his way down the driveway to his own vehicle, Ryder considered his options. For him, walking away wasn't one of them.

He was accustomed to home owners opening their doors wide and inviting him and his *Ryder to the Rescue* crew to come inside—not just happy but grateful to see him. Because it was his job to fix other contractors' mistakes, to finish the projects that do-it-yourselfers gave up on doing. In sum, he gave people what they wanted and they were appreciative of his time and efforts. They hugged him and sent him thank-you cards. They were never dismissive or disinterested.

Clearly Lauryn Schulte didn't understand what was at stake here, so he knocked on her door again.

There was no response.

He knew she was home, and she knew that he knew she was home, and thinking about that began to piss *him* off.

He knocked once more, and once more she ignored him.

But the little girl pushed back the curtains at the front window and waved to him. Something about her looked vaguely familiar—or maybe she just looked like most little girls of a similar age, even if he didn't know what that age might be.

He lifted a hand and waved back.

She smiled and twin dimples creased her cheeks. She really was a cute kid. Through the glass, he heard her mother say something. Though he couldn't decipher the actual words, the message was clear enough when the child gave one last wave before the curtains fell back into place over the window.

He sat on the porch, mostly sheltered from the rain pounding down around him by the overhang, and waited.

As he did, he made a quick visual scan of the surrounding area. It was a decent neighborhood, showing some signs of age. Most of the houses were simple designs—primarily bungalows and two stories, between thirty and forty years old—but well kept, the lawns tidy, flower beds tended. There were no flowers in Mrs. Schulte's garden, only a few scraggly bushes and a plastic bucket and shovel likely intended for digging in beach sand rather than potting soil.

He heard a click behind him—the dead bolt releasing—then the sound of the door opening.

"Why are you sitting on my porch in the rain?" Lauryn asked wearily.

He stood up and turned. Though her sweetly curved mouth was unsmiling and her soft gray-green eyes were filled with suspicion, neither detracted from her beauty. But he'd known a lot of beautiful women, and he wasn't going to be distracted from his task by an unexpected tug of attraction.

"Because you didn't invite me to come inside," he responded.

"And I'm not going to," she said firmly.

"Let's start at the top again," he suggested, with a hopeful smile. "My name is Ryder Wallace—I'm the host of WNCC's home improvement show *Ryder to the Rescue*."

She was unimpressed. "That still doesn't explain what you're doing here."

"I'm here to discuss the details of the work you want done, and it would be really great if you'd let me come in out of the rain to talk about it."

Though she was still frowning, she finally stepped away from the door to allow him entry.

"Do you have any coffee?" he asked hopefully.

"I thought you wanted to talk."

He smiled again. "Talking over a cup of coffee in the kitchen is so much friendlier than standing in the foyer."

"You're right," she said, "but I'm not feeling particularly friendly."

The little girl, who had been hiding behind her mother, peeked out at him now. "You can have tea wif me," she offered.

Lauryn sighed. "Kylie, what did Mama tell you about strangers?"

But the little girl shook her head. "He gived me flowers."

Ryder looked at the mom for an explanation, but she seemed equally confused by her daughter's statement.

"At the weddin'," Kylie clarified.

"My sister's wedding," he guessed, because it was the only one he'd attended recently.

Lauryn's puzzlement gave way to speculation. "Are you telling me that Avery Wallace is your sister?"

He nodded, confirming his relationship to the obstetrician who had recently married Justin Garrett, another doctor at Charisma's Mercy Hospital.

"Okay," she finally—reluctantly—relented. "I guess I can offer you a cup of coffee."

"Were you at the wedding?" he asked, following mother and daughter through the hallway to the kitchen he recognized from the photos she'd submitted with her application.

She shook her head. "No. Zachary—" she glanced at the baby in the playpen, playing with colorful plastic rings "—was running a bit of a fever, so we stayed home. Kylie went with my parents. And when you caught the bride's bouquet—"

"Avery threw it at me," he felt compelled to point out in his defense. "It was an automatic reflex."

She shrugged, as if the details were unimportant, and set a filter into the basket of the coffeemaker on the counter—the only modern appliance visible in the whole room.

"And when you caught the bouquet," she said again, measuring grounds into the filter, "you gave the flowers to Kylie."

He looked at the little girl in the frilly nightgown and finally remembered. "You were wearing a dark blue dress?"

Kylie smiled and nodded.

"Then you must be related to Justin," he said to Lauryn.

"He's my cousin," she admitted. "Our fathers are brothers."

"Small world," he mused, wondering if the loose familial connection would help or hinder his case.

"Small town," she corrected, handing him the mug of coffee. "Cream or sugar?"

"Sugar, please."

She offered him the sugar bowl and a spoon so he could fix it the way he liked it.

As he did, he asked, "Why do I get the impression that you changed your mind about being on the show?"

"What are you talking about?"

He frowned at the genuine bafflement in her tone. "You applied for a Room Rescue from *Ryder to the Rescue*."

"My sister Tristyn is addicted to the show, but I don't think I've ever seen it," she told him. "I don't have time to watch a lot of television, and when I do, it's usually *Nick Jr.*"

He acknowledged that with a nod. "So was it your sister who told you about the Room Rescue contest?"

She shook her head. "I honestly don't know anything about a contest."

He pulled the application out of his pocket and passed it across the table as Kylie tugged on her mother's arm and whispered something close to her ear.

"Yes, you can go up to your room to play for a little while," she said, and her daughter skipped off.

Lauryn unfolded the page and immediately began skimming the document, her brows furrowing. She finished reading and set the page down. "Well, it's all true," she admitted. "Except that I didn't send this in."

He pointed to the signature box. "That's not you?"

"It's my name—and a pretty good replica of my signature, which leads me to believe that one or both of my sisters filled out the application."

He winced. "The application is a contract, so I'll pretend I didn't hear you say that, then my director won't want to get our legal department involved."

"Can't you just tell him that I changed my mind?" she suggested hopefully.

"I don't understand," he admitted. "Most people would be thrilled by the prospect of a brand-new kitchen."

She looked around the dull and outdated room. "Rob had plans for this space—new cabinets, granite counter, ceramic floor."

"We can certainly consult with your husband about the design," he offered, attempting to appease her.

She shook her head. "He's not here."

"When will he be back?"

"Well, he left nine months ago, so I don't expect him to return anytime soon."

"I'm sorry," he said automatically.

"Don't be," she said. "I'm not."

He took a moment to regroup and reconsider his strategy. "Then forget about his plans," he urged. "What do *you* want?"

Lauryn stood up to lift the now-fussing baby from his playpen. "I don't even know where to begin to answer that question."

Opening a cupboard, she took a cookie out of a box. The little guy reached for it eagerly and immediately began gnawing on it.

Kylie returned to the kitchen, walking past the table to the back door, where she shoved her feet into a pair of pink rain boots.

"I told you we could go to the park later," Lauryn reminded her daughter. "You're supposed to be playing in your room now."

The little girl nodded. "But it's wainin' in the castle."

Her mother frowned. "What do you mean 'it's raining in the castle'? The rain is outside, honey."

This time Kylie shook her head. "The wain's on my bed."

Lauryn pushed back her chair and, with the baby propped on her hip, raced down the narrow hallway and up the stairs.

Instinctively, Ryder followed.

She stood in the doorway of what was obviously her daughter's bedroom, staring at the water dripping from the ceiling onto the little girl's bed. And puddling beside her tall dresser. And in front of her closet.

Her bottom lip trembled as she fought to hold back the tears that now filled her eyes.

"Why's it wainin' inside, Mama?" Kylie asked.

"Because it wasn't a crappy enough day already," her mother muttered in weary response.

The little girl gasped. "You said a bad word."

"Yes, I did," she admitted.

"Where's your attic access?" Ryder asked her.

"My bedroom," she told him.

He followed her across the hall. She reached for the loop of white rope in the ceiling. Of course, even on tiptoe, her fingertips barely brushed the rope. He easily reached up to grasp the handle and pull down the stairs.

She looked up into the yawning darkness overhead. "I can't remember the last time I was up there," she admitted. "I don't even know if there's a light."

Even if there was, there was also water coming into the house and Ryder wasn't willing to take a chance on forty-year-old wiring. Instead, he pulled the flashlight from his tool belt, switched on the beam and began his ascent.

It was a fairly typical attic—with a wide-planked floor over the joists of the ceiling below so that he didn't have to worry about where he stepped. A tiny window at each end illuminated dust and cobwebs along with various boxes and some old furniture. He lifted the beam of light to the ceiling and noted the distinct wet patches that showed him where the rain was coming in.

He walked back to the access and called down to Lauryn. "Can you get me some old towels and buckets?"

"I only have one bucket," she told him.

"Wastebaskets or big pasta pots would work."

She nodded and disappeared to gather the required items while he continued his inspection of the attic ceiling.

"Why's it wainin' in the castle?"

The little voice, so unexpected and close behind him, made Ryder start.

"How did you get up here?" he demanded.

"I comed up the ladder," Kylie told him.

"I'm not sure your mom would want you climbing up ladders when she's not around."

"Why's it wainin' in the castle?" she asked again, a little impatiently this time.

"There's a hole in the roof," he explained, shining the light to show her where the water was coming in. "Actually, a few holes."

"You fix it?"

"Yeah, I can fix it," he said, and was rewarded with a smile that lit up the dim space and tugged at his heart.

"Kylie?" her mother shouted out from below, her voice panicky. "Kylie—where are you?"

"She's with me," Ryder called down, taking the little girl's hand to lead her back to the stairs.

Though Kylie had bravely made the climb up, the sudden death grip on his hand as they approached the opening warned him that she wasn't so keen about going down again.

"Do you want me to carry you?" he asked her.

Eyes wide, she nodded quickly.

Her arms immediately went around his neck when he scooped her up. And in that moment, that quickly, he fell for this brave and terrified little girl who so openly and willingly placed her trust in him.

Lauryn was reaching for her daughter even before he hit the last step, simultaneously hugging her tight and chastising her for disappearing. Ryder left her to that task while he picked up the items she'd gathered and returned to the attic.

It didn't take him long to direct the water from the various points of origin into the bucket and pots she'd supplied. Of course, that would only contain the rain, not stop it from coming in, but it was the best he could do for now.

When he came back downstairs, the baby had fallen asleep in his crib, Kylie was dressed and Lauryn was tying a ribbon in her daughter's hair. The puddles in the little girl's room had been mopped up, and plastic bowls put in place to capture any more water that leaked through.

Ryder took a moment to look around the room and appreciate the detailed painting on the walls that he'd barely noticed earlier. "Did you do this?"

Lauryn shook her head. "My sister did."

"It's incredible," he said.

"Jordyn is incredibly talented." She looked worriedly at the ceiling, where a dragon flew in the sky above the castle walls.

"It won't take much to touch up after the roof is fixed."

She nodded, though she didn't look reassured.

In fact, she looked as if she had the weight of the enormous dragon—and entire fairy-tale kingdom—resting on her narrow shoulders.

Damn, but he'd always been a sucker for a damsel in distress. And this damsel had a lot more distress than she seemed to be able to handle right now.

"In the interim, I could put tarps up on the roof to give you some extra protection," he offered.

But she squared her shoulders and turned to face him. "You've done enough already, thanks. And now, I really need you to go so that I can run my errands."

"Do you want me to recommend a good roofer?"

"No, thanks," she said. "I've got someone who came out once before."

"If your roof is still leaking, maybe you need somebody different," he suggested.

Her cheeks flushed. "He warned me that I would need to redo the whole roof."

"When was that?"

"April," she admitted.

"You were told, *five months ago*, that you needed a new roof, and you haven't done anything about it?" he asked incredulously.

She lifted her chin. "Not that I owe you any explanations, but I've been kind of busy trying to take care of my two kids and run the business that my husband walked away from."

"I wasn't implying that you should have climbed up onto the roof to strip and reapply shingles yourself, just that you should have scheduled the work to be done."

"And I would have," she said. "But in my experience, most people generally want to be paid for the work that they do."

And that was when he realized she hadn't been neglectful— she couldn't afford a new roof. Obviously, he didn't have any details about her financial situation, but he suspected that she'd just given him the leverage he needed to secure her cooperation for the show.

"That's usually the way those things work," he acknowledged. "But, sometimes, other arrangements can be made."

She narrowed her gaze. "I really think you should go now."

He held up his hands in mock surrender. "I wasn't suggesting anything inappropriate," he assured her. "It seems apparent that, as much as you'd like a new kitchen, there are other issues that require more immediate attention."

"Your observational skills must be why your name is in the title of the show," she remarked dryly.

"And I know you're reluctant to participate in the show—"

"I'm not reluctant," she denied. "I'm refusing."

"But why?"

"Because this isn't a television studio, it's my home," she told him. "Maybe there are some things that I'd like to change and other things that need to be changed—like the roof—but I have no desire to open up the doors and let your camera crews dissect my personal space for your television viewers."

"You'd get a brand-new kitchen," he reminded her.

She shook her head stubbornly. "I don't need a new kitchen that desperately."

"But you do need a new roof—and I can get you that, too. In fact, we can specify whatever home improvements you want in the contract."

For the first time, he saw a hint of interest in her gray-green eyes. "You can really get my roof fixed?"

"Yes, I can," he assured her.

"What will it cost me?"

"Not a dime. We have a generous budget, as well as numerous sponsors and endorsement deals that will cover everything. *If*," he said, clearly emphasizing the word, "you agree to appear on the show."

He could see her weighing the pros and cons in her mind. In the end, practicality triumphed.

"When can you start?"

Chapter Three

Ryder left shortly after that, promising to have the contract revised to reflect the terms of their verbal agreement.

Lauryn still had some concerns, but she pushed them aside and packed the kids into the van to take them to her parents' house before her appointment with Howard Greenbaum, the loans manager at the bank. Howard and her father were old friends and she'd known the man since she was a little girl. She also knew that Howard would never let that long-term friendship affect any decisions that had to be made on the job—a fact that he confirmed before she left the bank.

When Lauryn returned to her childhood home, Zachary was napping in his playpen and Kylie was playing with some of her mother's old dolls in front of the television in the living room—keeping Grandpa company while he watched his favorite afternoon game shows. Looking at her children now, everything seemed so normal, so right. But she was suddenly and painfully aware of how quickly their situation could change.

Still, she was lucky. She knew that no matter what else happened, her parents would never let her kids go hungry or sleep on a park bench. And while there was undoubtedly some comfort in that realization, she wanted to provide for her own family—even if she was becoming increasingly doubtful that she could.

"Is everything okay?" Susan Garrett asked when Lauryn made her way to the kitchen, where her mother was tidying up after baking cookies.

She could only shake her head.

"Do you want to talk about it?" her mother prompted.

She shook her head again, then let out a sigh.

"Actually I do," she admitted. "But if I talk about it, I'll fall apart, and I don't want Kylie to see me fall apart."

Susan pulled a glass from the cupboard, filled it with milk, then set the drink and a plate of chocolate-chip cookies on the table and instructed her daughter to sit.

So Lauryn did. And, unable to resist, she reached for a cookie and broke off a piece. The still-warm morsel flooded her mouth with the flavor of her childhood and made her yearn—almost desperately—for those simpler times when her mother could make all of her troubles go away. But she was the mother now; she had to handle her own troubles and make things right for her children.

"Are there problems at The Locker Room?" Susan asked, aware that Lauryn was trying to pull the sporting goods store back from the brink of financial disaster.

She managed a wry smile. "Aren't there always?"

"Then something else—something more—is weighing on your mind," her mother noted. "Have you heard from Rob?"

She shook her head. "Not a single word. And believe me, that's a relief not a disappointment."

"I can understand that," Susan acknowledged. "What I can't understand is how he could walk away from his children. Regardless of what happened between the two of you, he's their father."

"Apparently, that title doesn't mean the same thing to all men," Lauryn noted.

"Has Kylie asked about him lately?"

She shook her head. "Not in a while."

"Maybe that's for the best," her mother said.

"I'm sure she misses him," Lauryn said, then reconsidered. "Or maybe not. Even when he was around, he wasn't much of a hands-on dad."

"So if you're not worried about Rob," Susan prompted.

"I've just got a lot on my mind."

"If there's anything I can do to help, you know—"

"I do know," Lauryn interjected. "But you already do so much."

Her mother seemed genuinely surprised by that. "What do I do?"

"You look after Kylie and Zachary whenever I need you to."

"Honey, that's not a favor to you but a treat for me," Susan told her.

"I love you for saying that, but I know my kids—they're not always a treat."

"They are for their grandparents," her mother insisted.

Lauryn managed a smile. "They're so lucky to have both of you. *I'm* so lucky to have both of you."

Susan lifted a hand to brush her daughter's bangs away from her eyes. "Can you stay for dinner?"

Of course, they could. And no doubt, whatever her mother had planned for the evening meal would be better than the meat loaf Lauryn had thrown together that morning. But her parents had already been with the kids for four hours, fed them lunch and probably numerous snacks.

"Thanks, but I've got dinner ready to go in the oven at home."

"We're having roast pork with fingerling potatoes and green beans," Susan said in a final attempt at persuasion.

"Enjoy," Lauryn said, kissing her mother's cheek.

When the rain finally stopped early in the afternoon, Ryder loaded up the necessary supplies and headed back to the Schulte residence. It wouldn't take him long to tack down the tarps, and since Lauryn had said she had errands to run, he expected to complete the task and be gone before she returned.

He didn't quite make it. He was securing his ladder into the bed of his truck when she pulled an aging minivan into the driveway beside his truck.

The Garretts were one of the wealthiest and most well-known families in Charisma. Of course, Lauryn's last name was different, which was why he hadn't immediately made the connection, but as soon as Kylie had mentioned the flowers and the wedding, he'd started to put the pieces together into a more complete picture. But there were still big, gaping holes in the form of the ancient van, leaking roof and outdated kitchen. He finished the tying down while she got the kids out of the vehicle and decided that, sooner or later, he would fill those holes.

He noticed that she'd changed out of the yellow T-shirt and jeans into a slim-fitting navy skirt and jacket and tucked her feet into high-heeled sandals. He also noticed that she had some pretty nice curves beneath the buttoned-up suit.

He shook his head, as if that might dislodge the unwelcome thought from his brain. She was his client—and if he expected to be able to work with her, he had no business ogling her. Not to mention that she really wasn't his type. He preferred uncomplicated women and simple relationships—a single mother, no matter how beautiful and desirable, didn't fit that criteria.

"What are you doing here, Mr. Wallace?" she asked.

"Ryder," he reminded her.

"What are you doing here, *Ryder*?"

He smiled at the pique in her tone. "I took advantage of the break in the weather to put some tarps up."

Her gaze shifted to the roof of the house. "You didn't have to do that," she protested.

"I wanted to make sure you wouldn't get any more rain in the castle," he said, winking at Kylie. "And give the wood a chance to dry out so that it will be ready when the roofers are."

"You're really going to get my roof fixed?"

"I said I would," he reminded her.

She nodded. "Rob used to say a lot of things, too," she admitted. "But he didn't follow through on many of them."

"Home renovations aren't as easy as a lot of people think," he said, even as he wondered what had gone wrong in her marriage and if she was still hung up on her ex-husband.

"Well, thanks for putting up the tarps." She started to move past him toward the house.

"Since we're going to be spending a lot of time together over the next few weeks, you might want to ease up on the hostility a little," he suggested.

"I'm not—" She blew out a breath and shook her head. "I'm sorry. It's been a really bad day and I'm taking it out on you, and after you went out of your way to help me out—which I do appreciate."

"You're welcome."

She started toward the door again, then hesitated. "Are you one of those people who drinks coffee all day?"

He smiled. "Is that a roundabout way of offering me a cup?"

She shrugged. "It seems the least I can do—if you're interested."

Yeah, he was interested, and apparently in more than just the hot beverage she was offering. The tug of attraction he felt for the home owner was more than a little disconcerting because, aside from the fact that single mothers weren't his type, Ryder had a very strict rule against mixing business with pleasure. If he was smart, he'd say, *Thanks, but no thanks*, climb into his truck and head home. Maybe he'd

even return Holly's call and accept her offer of dinner—
and dessert. His occasional friend-with-benefits was fun
and single and, most importantly, she'd never asked for
anything more than he was willing to give. Yes, he should
definitely call Holly back.

"Coffee would be great," he said instead.

Lauryn led him into the house. After setting Zachary in
his playpen, she started the coffee brewing.

"I wanna dwink, too," Kylie said, retrieving a juice box
from the fridge.

"Okay," Lauryn agreed, unwrapping the straw and inserting it into the top of the box.

The little girl took a sip, then set it aside. "Cookie?"

This time her mother shook her head. "You already had
cookies at Grandma's."

So Kylie turned her attention to Ryder. "Cookie?" she
asked hopefully, adding a smile for good measure.

He chuckled. "Sorry—I don't have any cookies."

The little girl pouted.

"Your coloring book and crayons are still on the table
in the living room," Lauryn told her daughter.

With an exaggerated sigh, Kylie turned toward the living room.

"You're going to have your hands full with that one,"
Ryder said to Lauryn.

"They're full enough already," she admitted, setting a
mug of coffee and the sugar in front of him.

"How old is she?"

"Three and a half."

"And the little guy?" he asked, glancing at the playpen
where the baby had managed to pull himself to his feet and
was gnawing on the frame.

Lauryn's gaze followed his as she sat down across from
him with her own mug. "Seven months and—as you can
see—teething."

He frowned. "Didn't you say your husband left nine months ago?"

"I did," she confirmed.

"It must have been hard on you—having the baby without him," he noted.

She shrugged. "My sister Tristyn was there."

"The one who forged your signature on the application?"

"I thought we were going to pretend I didn't tell you that."

"We were," he acknowledged. "But then I thought that we might be able to use your sisters in the introductory segment—put them in front of the cameras and let them explain why they wanted this renovation for you."

"They'd probably love that," she said. "But Tristyn's job requires her to travel a lot, so it would depend on when you planned to film the segment."

"Monday," he told her.

"Monday—as in five days from now?"

"Is that a problem?"

"No," she admitted. "I mean—I'm still not entirely comfortable with this, but I guess Monday is as good a day as any to begin."

"Do you think your sisters can be here?" he asked.

She shrugged again. "It shouldn't be a problem. Besides, they owe me—even if they don't know it yet."

"Hopefully, by the time we're done, you'll be thanking rather than blaming them," he told her.

"Hopefully," she agreed, then sighed when she saw Kylie slip back into the room and open a cupboard beside the fridge. "No more cookies."

"But I'm hungwy."

Lauryn stood up and moved to the stove, twisting a knob to turn it on. "Dinner won't be too long," she promised.

She took a yogurt tube out of the fridge and snipped off the top.

"Is Mister Wyder gonna have dinner wif us?" Kylie asked, taking the tube from her.

"Oh. Um." She felt her cheeks flush as she delicately tried to wiggle out of the awkward position her daughter had put her in. "I'm sure Ryder already has plans for dinner."

Kylie turned to him. "Do you?"

"Actually, I don't have plans," he told her.

"You have dinner wif us?" she asked again.

His gaze shifted from the little girl to her mother. "What are you cooking?"

"Meat loaf," she told him, taking the already prepared pan from the refrigerator and sliding it into the oven. "With a side of mac and cheese and salad."

She hadn't planned on adding macaroni and cheese to the meal, but she wasn't sure that the meat loaf and salad would stretch far enough to feed all of them if he decided to stay.

"Sounds good," he decided.

She eyed him skeptically. "Really?"

He smiled, and she felt an unexpected warmth spread through her veins. "Well, it sounds a lot better than the pizza I probably would have ordered at home."

"I like pizza," Kylie told him.

"So do I," he admitted. "But it gets kind of monotonous when you eat it four or five times a week."

"What's mon-tin-us?"

"Monotonous," he said again, enunciating clearly. "And it means boring."

Lauryn took a pot out of the cupboard and filled it with water, then set it on the stove to boil.

Although she would have been able to get two meals out of the meat loaf if she was only feeding herself and the kids, she was glad he was staying. She'd had a really crappy day and while she certainly wouldn't have sought out any company, she was grateful for the distraction. Because as long as Ryder was there, she didn't have to think about how spectacularly she'd screwed up her life or try to figure out how she was supposed to put all of the broken pieces back together again. As an added bonus, he was great with her kids—and, she admitted to herself, really nice to look at.

"Can I help with anything?" Ryder offered.

She shook her head. "The salad is in the fridge, the meat loaf is in the oven, and the mac and cheese will only take ten minutes after the water boils. But if you'll excuse me for a minute, I'm just going to run upstairs to change into something more forgiving of sticky fingers."

Ryder nodded.

She was gone less than three minutes, exchanging her dry-clean-only business attire for a comfortable pair of faded jeans and a peasant-style blouse. When she returned to the kitchen, he was refilling his mug of coffee from the pot.

She picked up her own abandoned cup and sat down across from him.

Ryder ran his fingers over the surface of the table. He had really great hands—a workman's hands—strong and capable. "I noticed you've got a lot of quality furniture inside this house with the leaky roof, falling-down porch and ugly kitchen."

"I took advantage of the employee discount at Garrett Furniture," she told him.

He lifted a brow. "Not the family discount?"

"I didn't think it would take you too long to figure it out after Kylie mentioned Justin and Avery's wedding."

"Did you want it to remain a secret?" he asked.

She sipped her coffee. "No. But I don't want the Garrett name used on the show."

"Why not?"

Because she was embarrassed enough about her financial situation, and the last thing she wanted was to cause embarrassment to her family. She knew it wasn't easy for her parents to overlook all of the work that needed to be done in her home. More than once, her father had offered to call a handyman friend to fix the leaky plumbing in the kitchen, to replace some questionable boards in the front porch, to secure the wobbly ceiling fan in the master bedroom. Every time, Lauryn had refused because her husband had promised to take care of the problems.

It was harder to turn away her cousins when they showed up at the door, as Andrew and Nathan had done a few times. It was thanks to them that she had a secure handrail leading to the laundry room in the basement and shelves in the nursery. And the new locks on the doors were courtesy of Daniel, who had installed them within hours of learning that Rob had walked out on his family. Not that she intended to admit any of that to the man seated across the table from her now.

"Can't you just respect my wishes on this?" she finally said.

He considered for a minute, then nodded. "Okay."

"Well, that was easy," she said both grateful and a little dubious.

"Did you expect me to be difficult?"

"You weren't nearly as agreeable when I asked you to get off my property this morning," she reminded him.

"I know you're not thrilled about being part of the show, but everything will go much more smoothly if you accept that we're on the same team," he told her.

"Are we?"

"Why do you doubt it?"

She shrugged. "A lot of so-called reality TV shows are all about the conflict and drama."

"Maybe you should watch a few episodes of *Ryder to the Rescue* before you sign the contract," he advised.

"Maybe I will," she agreed.

"In the meantime—" he nodded toward the stove "—your water is boiling."

She hurried to open the window above the sink, to let the steamy air escape, because the range fan didn't work. Then she opened the box of macaroni and dumped the noodles into the pot.

Ryder found plates and cutlery and set the table. She started to tell him that she would do it, because she was accustomed to doing everything on her own, then she decided that it was nice—at least this once—to have some help. Besides, while she finished the preparations for dinner, she was able to watch him move around her kitchen— and she really liked watching him move.

After making the pasta sauce, she called Kylie for dinner, then dished up her food while the little girl was washing up. She cut up some meat for Zachary and added a spoonful of macaroni, then slid his plate into the freezer while she settled him into his high chair and buckled the belt around his middle. Kylie had already climbed into her booster seat and was shoveling spoonfuls of macaroni and cheese into her mouth.

"Ketchup, please."

Lauryn grabbed the bottle of ketchup from the fridge, shook it up and squirted a dollop onto her daughter's plate—close to but not touching the meat—then set the bottle on the table.

"Umm umm," Zachary was making his hungry noises and reaching toward his sister's plate.

"Yours is just cooling off," Lauryn promised, offering a sippy cup of milk to tide him over.

He immediately put the spout in his mouth, took a drink, then tossed the cup aside. "Umm umm," he demanded.

Holding back a sigh, she bent to retrieve it, but Ryder had already scooped it off the floor and set it on the table.

It was then she noticed that his fork was still beside his plate, his food untouched.

"Please don't wait for me," Lauryn told him. "Your dinner will get cold if you do."

"No colder than yours," he pointed out.

She opened the door of the freezer to check on Zachary's meal. "I'm used to it. Sometimes the kids are finished before I get a chance to start."

Satisfied with the temperature of the baby's food, she set the plate in front of him. Zachary, like his sister, did not stand on ceremony but immediately shoved a hand into the macaroni.

Lauryn uncurled his fingers and wrapped them around the handle of the spoon she'd given to him. He held on to the utensil, then used the other hand to pick up a piece of meat. Shaking her head, she sat down at her plate and wiped her fingers on a napkin.

Only when she was seated did Ryder pick up his own fork. Not even her husband had ever waited for her to sit down before digging into his own meal, but she pushed that memory aside.

She'd taken the first bite of her dinner when the sky suddenly grew dark and she heard the rumble of thunder in the distance. But it was distant—far, far away, she assured herself, stabbing her fork into a piece of meat just as the skies opened up and rain poured down.

She pushed the meat around until Ryder reached across the table and put his hand over hers. She jolted at the unexpected contact, her fork slipping from her fingers and clattering against the edge of her plate, but he didn't pull his hand away.

"The tarps will hold," he told her.

She nodded, grateful for his reassurance and a little unnerved that this man, whom she'd met only hours earlier, had so easily followed the direction of her thoughts. Even more unnerving was the way her skin had warmed and her pulse had leaped in response to his touch.

She slowly drew her hand away. "Did you want more meat loaf?"

"I wouldn't mind another slice."

She pushed away from the table and reached for his plate.

"I can get it," he told her.

"More milk, please," Kylie said, lifting up her empty cup.

"I can get that, too," Ryder said, when she started to rise again.

Settling back in her seat, Lauryn forced herself to take another bite of her dinner. She blamed the rain for her loss of appetite, because she was worried about potential new leaks.

But she was more worried about the sudden and unexpected tingles she'd felt all the way to her toes when Ryder touched her.

Chapter Four

Meat loaf and macaroni and cheese seemed to Ryder like a traditional family meal, but he couldn't be certain. He'd grown up in a family that was anything but traditional, with two parents who spent more time at their respective jobs than at home and happily abdicated responsibility for the upbringing of their children to the nanny.

He and Avery had been lucky there, because Hennie had been wonderful. Right up until Ryder was twelve and Avery fifteen, when George and Cristina—long divorced but still making such decisions together—had concluded that their children didn't need a caregiver anymore.

Spending time with Lauryn and her children was almost like entering a whole new world—and not one in which he felt entirely comfortable. He was accustomed to eating alone, and usually in front of the television. Except when his sister took pity on him and invited him over for a meal. He appreciated those invitations for a lot of reasons, not the least of which was that Avery was a fabulous cook. He also suspected that those invitations would be fewer and further between now that his sister had a husband and a baby.

By the time Zachary had finished all of his meat and noodles, his face and fingers were covered with cheese sauce. He even had bits of ground beef and macaroni in his hair.

"I think someone needs a bath," Lauryn said, when she took his empty plate away.

"Zach!" Kylie declared.

"Well, Zachary's going to get his first," her mother agreed.

"Why don't Kylie and I tidy up the kitchen while you clean up the little guy?" Ryder suggested.

"You don't have to do that," she protested.

"I don't mind," he told her, because it seemed only fair that he should do something to show his appreciation for the delicious meal. On the other hand, he couldn't deny there was a part of him that was itching to make his escape from this unfamiliar yet somehow temptingly cozy situation.

The whole dinner scene had been a little too domestic for him—and a lot outside his comfort zone. Being around the sexy single mom and her adorable kids was creating some unfamiliar and unwelcome feelings.

Attraction was a simple emotion, and he had no trouble recognizing and acknowledging his attraction to Lauryn. It was the other stuff that was getting all tangled up inside of him. Because aside from the fact that she turned him on, there were a lot of reasons that he simply liked her. She was smart and warm and kind, and it was readily obvious that she doted on her kids.

And that was the crux of the problem right there—she had children. Children were a complication and Ryder didn't want complications in his life. At least he never had before.

But since his sister had gotten married and had had her baby and he'd seen how those new bonds had enriched her life, he'd begun to wonder if there wasn't something to be said for familial connections.

He'd always admired Avery's intelligence and drive and ambition. But since she'd fallen in love with Justin Garrett, he saw something in her that he hadn't before: joy. It was almost as if there had been a piece missing from her life, but she'd never known it until she met him.

Ryder wasn't looking for anyone to complete him. He was perfectly content with his life. Yet, spending time with

Lauryn and Kylie and Zachary tonight, he found himself wondering if maybe he wasn't ready for something more.

Uncomfortable with those feelings, he pushed them aside to be considered at a later date—or preferably not at all.

"I think you should stop arguing with me," he said to Lauryn now, "and get Zachary in the bath before he falls asleep in his high chair."

She shifted her attention to the baby, whose chin was against his chest, his eyelids visibly drooping. "That's a good plan," she agreed, unhooking the tray and then lifting him out of his seat.

As soon as she picked him up, Zachary rubbed his face against her shoulder, leaving a smear of cheese sauce on her shirt. Lauryn either didn't notice or didn't care, and for some reason he found that incredibly appealing.

Most of the women he'd dated over the past few years had been preoccupied with their clothes and hair and makeup, and he found it tiresome to date a woman who rushed off to reapply her lipstick after a meal or was constantly fluffing her hair or adjusting her hemlines. Of course, he'd never dated someone with kids, and he suspected it was natural for a woman's priorities to change when she became a mother—his own being an obvious exception.

Kids were loud and messy and demanding, and he already knew that was true of both Kylie and Zachary. They were also innocent and trusting and adorable. And while he'd been immediately charmed by the little girl who was full of energy and curiosity, and undoubtedly intrigued by the little boy who seemed to see everything but say nothing, he decided that it would be smart to take a step back. Maybe even two.

Because Lauryn and Kylie and Zachary were a family, and he was a contented bachelor with no desire to change that status.

Wasn't he?

* * *

At eleven o'clock on Saturday, Lauryn met both of her sisters at the Morning Glory Café for brunch. After Lauryn had married Rob, she'd discovered that she didn't get to see Jordyn and Tristyn nearly as often as she used to, and that was how the monthly "Sisters' Saturday" tradition began.

"I had an interesting visitor Wednesday morning," Lauryn said, sprinkling pepper on the home fries that accompanied her scrambled eggs and sausage.

"Who?" Jordyn asked, drowning her pancakes in syrup.

"Can't you guess?"

Tristyn stabbed a piece of melon with her fork. "Is it someone that we know?"

"It turns out that there is a loose familial connection."

"Now you've piqued my curiosity," Jordyn admitted.

"Ryder Wallace."

Tristyn's fork slipped from her fingers. *"Ryder to the Rescue?"*

Lauryn nodded. "Apparently the home renovation expert is Justin's new wife's brother."

"I knew that," Tristyn admitted, picking up her utensil again.

"But why was he at your house?" Jordyn asked, her tone equal parts curious and cautious as she cut into a pancake.

"That's what I wondered—and then he told me that my application was selected as one of the grand prize winners in WNCC's Room Rescue contest."

"Oh, my God!" Tristyn practically squealed with delight. "That is *so* awesome."

"And surprising, considering that I never submitted an application," Lauryn pointed out. "In fact, I'd never even heard of the contest. So imagine my surprise when he showed me the application with my name and signature on it."

Her sisters exchanged a look.

"Actually, that's kind of a funny story," Jordyn began.

"I can't wait to hear it," Lauryn told her.

"Obviously you know it was us," Tristyn said, stirring her yogurt and granola. "And we're not going to apologize, because somebody had to do something."

"So why didn't you tell me?"

"Because we never expected that our—*your*—application would actually be chosen," Jordyn admitted.

"But it was," she pointed out. "And I felt like a complete idiot when Ryder Wallace showed up at my door and I had absolutely no idea why he was there."

"I can see how that might have been a little awkward," Jordyn conceded.

"It was more than a little awkward."

"Is he as hot in person as he is on TV?" Tristyn asked curiously.

She'd followed Ryder's advice and decided to watch a few episodes of his show. As a result, she could answer her sister's question sincerely. "Much hotter."

"Damn, I wish I'd been there."

Lauryn couldn't deny that there was an indescribable something about the man that any woman would find appealing. He was strong and sexy and incredibly charismatic, and after only a few hours in his company, she was halfway toward a serious infatuation. Of course, after being married to a man who didn't know how to hang a picture on the wall, it probably wasn't surprising that she'd be intrigued by a take-charge guy who owned his tools and knew how to use them. "You can be there Monday."

"What's Monday?" Jordyn asked, smiling her thanks to the waitress who refilled her mug with coffee.

"The whole crew is coming to the house on Monday and Ryder wants the two of you to explain, on camera, why you submitted the application for me," she told her sisters.

"Then he is going to remodel your kitchen?"

"And fix a few other things," she acknowledged.

"Why don't you sound more excited?" Tristyn asked. "You're finally going to get rid of those ugly cupboards and even uglier linoleum."

She swallowed a mouthful of eggs. "With the added bonus of a bunch of strangers traipsing through my house."

"They're not going to be there forever," Tristyn pointed out. "Just long enough to give you a fabulous kitchen makeover—which you've wanted since you bought that place."

"I know. But I thought…" She sighed. "I thought Rob and I would do it."

There was silence for a moment before Jordyn cautiously asked, "Do you…miss him?"

"No," she replied, a little ashamed to admit that it was true. But her ex-husband had stopped being a factor in her life long before he walked out on their marriage.

"Good."

Her eyes widened in response to the vehemence in her sister's tone.

"I'm sorry," Jordyn said. "But none of us ever thought he was good enough for you."

"I thought he was perfect—and I felt so lucky that he picked me."

"You *are* lucky," Tristyn said. "Because you got two wonderful kids out of the deal."

"And because you've got the two best sisters in the world," Jordyn chimed in.

Lauryn smiled. "You're right—on both counts."

"And you get to spend the afternoon at Serenity Spa with those sisters," Jordyn added.

She shook her head regretfully. "I'm sorry, I can't go today."

"What do you mean—you can't go?" Tristyn demanded.

"I don't have the time…or the money," she admitted.

"It's a Garrett sisters' tradition," Jordyn reminded her. "And we're not letting you skip out on it—*again*."

Lauryn looked away. "I appreciate what you're trying to do, but I had an appointment at the bank on Wednesday and discovered that my financial situation is even more dismal than I realized."

"How dismal?" Tristyn asked gently.

"The business is mortgaged to the hilt."

"But you knew that," Jordyn reminded her. "That's why you should sell it, or let the bank take it and all of the headaches that go with it."

"I was starting to see the benefits of that plan," Lauryn admitted. "Until I found out the business also has a secured line of credit."

Her sisters exchanged another look, this one confirming that they'd both guessed how it was secured.

Jordyn winced. "Oh, no."

"The house," Tristyn whispered.

Lauryn nodded and pushed her plate away, her appetite gone.

"But how is that possible?" Jordyn wondered. "Wouldn't Rob have needed you to sign any paperwork?"

"Signatures can be forged," Tristyn reminded her, looking guilty because they'd done exactly that for the Room Rescue.

"They can," Lauryn agreed. "But he didn't forge my signature."

"You didn't—you *wouldn't*—jeopardize your home," Jordyn asserted.

"You're right—I wouldn't. At least not knowingly. But I did sign the papers," she admitted. "Based on the date of the application, when Kylie was about three months old."

"And colicky," Tristyn remembered.

She nodded. "I remember Rob came home early one

day with flowers. That should have been a clue, because he never came home early. Or with flowers.

"He told me that the business was doing well, but there was some new vendor—I don't remember whether it was equipment or apparel—but they were offering him exclusive retail rights for the area if he could commit to carrying the entire line in his inventory. He said that he'd been to the bank to get a loan and, because he was married, they wanted my signature, too."

She looked away, embarrassed and ashamed that she'd been so foolish. "I just signed the papers where he told me to. I didn't even read them.

"And now—" she fought against the tears that burned behind her eyes "—if I let the bank foreclose on the business, they could take the house, too."

"Then we need to come up with a plan to save the business," Jordyn said.

"And since my brain functions much better when I'm relaxed, we'll brainstorm some ideas after the spa."

"I already told you, I can't—"

"You can't say no," Tristyn interjected. "Mom made all the arrangements—*and* paid for it."

Lauryn sighed. "She shouldn't have done that."

"She didn't just do it for you, but for all of us. Because she knows how much we all enjoy the monthly ritual."

Because it was true—and because she loved being with the women who weren't just her sisters but her best friends—Lauryn gave up her protest.

Sweet Serenity Boutique & Spa was located in a renovated three-story Colonial Revival home in Northbrook, offering different services on different levels. The three sisters were on the lower level now, continuing their conversation as they perused the selection of polishes for their pedicures.

"I had no idea things were as bad as they are at the store," Lauryn confided. "Rob didn't let me see the books. He said it was because he wanted to take care of the business, to prove that he could take care of us."

"And a piss-poor job he did of both," Jordyn said bluntly.

Lauryn could only nod. "But I loved him. Maybe I was naive but, for a long time, I really did love him."

"I know you did," Tristyn said sympathetically.

"And you'll fall in love again," Jordyn told her.

"Jesus, I hope not," Lauryn said.

Her recently—and happily—married sister frowned. "Why would you say something like that?"

"Because I have no desire to repeat past mistakes." She sipped from her glass of cucumber-and-lime-infused spring water.

"You wouldn't," Jordyn said confidently. "Your relationship with Rob was a learning experience."

"Most importantly, I learned that I don't need a man to complete my life."

"As if he ever did," Tristyn remarked dryly.

"I didn't think I'd fall in love again," Jordyn confided. "I didn't think I could. And then I met Marco."

Lauryn couldn't help but smile at that. Marco Palermo had fallen head over heels for Jordyn and immediately set his sights on winning her heart—not an easy task. Four years earlier, Jordyn had been only weeks away from her wedding when her fiancé was killed in a car crash. As a result, she'd put up all kinds of barriers around her heart, refusing to let any man get too close. Until Marco.

While he wasn't at all the type of guy that Lauryn would have expected to steal her sister's heart, he was absolutely perfect for her. And they were perfect together. Lauryn was thrilled for both of them, and just a little bit envious. Because when she was with Jordyn and Marco, she realized that she'd never shared that kind of soul-deep love and connection with her own husband. But even as she lamented that fact, she wasn't looking for the same thing now—she had more important concerns.

"I just want my kids to be safe and happy and know that I love them."

"They are and they do," Jordyn assured her. "And while that's a legitimate and even admirable goal, you can't live your life for your children."

"Why don't we table this discussion until you have kids of your own?" Lauryn's tone was a little harsher than she'd intended, but neither of her sisters really understood what she was going through. They couldn't know the joy that filled her heart every time she looked at her children—or how much pressure she felt always trying to do what was best for them.

Thankfully, Jordyn wasn't offended by her sharp retort. And the thought of a baby—Marco's baby—was enough to make her deep green eyes go all misty and dreamy.

Unfortunately, Tristyn wasn't so easily distracted. "But what do *you* want?" she asked Lauryn.

I want to not worry that my bank card is going to be declined at the gas station because I just bought diapers and formula.

Not that she would admit as much to her sisters. Telling them about the business was one thing; whining about her personal finances was something else entirely. Her mistakes were her own and she was determined to fix them on her own. Of course, now that the bank had rejected her proposal, her options had gone from limited to almost nonexistent, but she wasn't ready to give up yet.

"Well, I have been thinking about making some changes in my life," she finally confided. "Maybe dyeing my hair to test the old adage about blondes having more fun."

Her sisters exchanged a look, and she knew they were

both thinking of Roxi—the perky blonde yoga instructor that Lauryn's husband had run off with.

"Or red," she said, because the color didn't matter as much as the change it would symbolize.

Tristyn shook her head. "Do you remember when I went red—or tried to? It took my stylist three hours to undo what I'd done, and he made me promise that if I ever wanted a drastic change I would stick to the color on my toes."

Lauryn looked at the pale pink and white polishes she'd chosen for her standard French pedicure.

Tristyn handed her the bottle of sparkly purple that she'd selected. "Go wild," she advised. "But in a way that won't do any long-term damage."

Lauryn looked at the color—equal parts intrigued and wary—and decided it was time to step out of her comfort zone. At least a little.

Chapter Five

Ryder loved his job. Of course, he'd prefer doing it without cameras recording him every step of the way, but he'd long ago accepted that as a necessary trade-off for being able to do the work he wanted to do. *Ryder to the Rescue* was currently one of the top-rated programs at WNCC, with a viewership that continued to grow with each successive season, but Virginia Gennings, the producer, wanted to keep the show fresh and the Room Rescue contest was her latest brainstorm.

Ryder's only real objection had come when Owen had delegated the task of choosing the contest winners to him. Three winners out of more than nine hundred entries from as far away as Texas and Seattle, with requests that ranged from a modest bathroom rehab to the complete reconfiguration of a floor plan. Owen's criteria for selection: stories that would appeal to viewers. Which meant that Ryder's original plan—to put all of the entries in a box and draw three at random—fell by the wayside as he spent hours reading application after application, sorting them into three distinct groupings of Maybe, No and No Way in Hell.

The majority of applications that went into the third pile were those that included naked pictures and explicit offers to express appreciation for his work when the cameras were gone or, in one notable case, with the cameras still rolling. The requests for free renovations by home owners who could well afford to pay for the work they wanted done landed in the No file. And then there was the Maybe group, from which he selected the winners.

Lauryn Schulte's application had appealed to him for several reasons, including her reference to the husband who didn't have time to do the renovation. Because the existence of a husband meant it was much less likely that he'd have to fend off the attention of an overzealous fan—a sticky situation that was occurring more frequently, seemingly in direct correlation to the show's increasing popularity.

According to Virginia, Ryder was the whole package—smart, sexy, strong and charismatic—and the female viewership of *Ryder to the Rescue* was so high because women trusted him and wanted to invite him into their homes. But Ryder liked to keep his private life private. Okay, so maybe he did date a lot of women, but he didn't dish about any of them and he made it clear that if they dished, they were history. As a result, for the first few seasons that the show was on the air, he'd mostly managed to keep a low profile.

Until the previous spring when he'd agreed to help Carl, one of his cameramen, build a deck on the back of his house. It was a simple project—a few hours' work on a sunny Saturday afternoon—and he hadn't hesitated when Carl asked if he was available. But it was a sunny and *hot* Saturday afternoon, and it hadn't taken him long to decide to strip off his T-shirt, as the other guys had also done. But he was the only one whose name was in the title of the show, and one of Carl's wife's friends had snapped a photo of #shirtlessRyder #summerdays and tweeted it to all of her friends. Apparently, the damn photo had gone viral, resulting in an endless discussion on social media about his #yummymuscles. He'd been appalled when Carl sheepishly brought it to his attention; Virginia had been delighted.

Since then, he'd been heralded not just as America's Hottest Handyman but also the Sexiest Man on WNCC. As a result, he'd become the target of much female admiration and media attention. And when WNCC launched the Room Rescue contest and had let it be known that all applications would be personally reviewed by the show's host, it was an opportunity for women to throw their pictures and phone numbers at Ryder in the hopes that, even if he didn't bring his construction crew to their homes, he might call.

He didn't.

The first project chosen was a master suite reno for a young couple near Anderson, South Carolina. The second assignment took his crew to Montana to finish a basement apartment for the college freshman son of a forty-seven-year-old widow in Miles City. The final winning application was Lauryn's.

Kitchen and bathroom renovations tended to be popular because they directly added to the value of a home, providing a good return on investment when it came time to resell the property. As a result, he'd done a lot of kitchen upgrades and remodels on the show. And while he wasn't overjoyed at the thought of starting yet another one, he was happy to finally be back home and able to sleep in his own bed.

Of course, he now knew that one of the main factors that had weighed in favor of Lauryn's application was no longer valid—the husband who had never found the time to do the renovation work was gone from her life. On the other hand, her two children obviously kept her busy enough that he didn't anticipate she would be an impediment to the project. She'd also shown less than zero interest in his celebrity status or #yummymuscles, making it clear that the only reason he was being allowed access to her house was that she desperately needed the new roof he'd promised to provide.

So what was it about the single mother that made her so unforgettable? With her long, dark hair, creamy skin, gray-green eyes and perfectly sculpted mouth, she was undeniably beautiful, but he'd met a lot of beautiful women over the years without becoming fixated on any of them.

Or maybe his fascination was with the kids rather than their mother. Because when he looked at Kylie and Zachary, he couldn't help but think about his sister and himself and the scars that were a result of growing up in a broken home. But Kylie and Zachary had one clear advantage over Avery and Ryder: an amazing mother who, despite the weight of so many responsibilities on her slender shoulders, did everything she could to ensure her children felt loved and secure.

And they were great kids. Zachary was an adorable and affectionate child with big blue eyes that seemed to take everything in. Kylie was a dynamo with silky dark curls and the sweetest Cupid's-bow mouth that was always quick to smile. She was fearless enough to climb up an open staircase into a dark attic, smart enough to be uncertain about making the trip back down and trusting enough to let him carry her out again.

Her mother wasn't nearly as trusting—but maybe she had reasons to be wary, having been abandoned by her husband when she was pregnant with their second child. Not only that, he'd gotten the impression that she hadn't heard from the guy since. Ryder shook his head, wondering what kind of person walked out on his family. But why did he care? Why did he wish he could make things better for her? Especially when she'd given no indication that she wanted or needed anyone to take care of her.

Whatever the reasons, he was suddenly looking forward to this project a lot more than he'd expected.

After the spa, Lauryn and her sisters browsed a few of the local shops. Jordyn oohed and aahed over the jewelry display in Zahara's but didn't buy anything. She'd always loved fun and funky accessories, but since her marriage to

Marco, she rarely wore anything more than the rings he'd put on her finger.

"Look at this," Jordyn said, holding up a hanger with a purple satin demi-cup bra with matching bikini panties.

"Why do you need something like that? You're practically still on your honeymoon," Tristyn noted.

"I wasn't thinking for me, but for Lauryn."

She eyed the lingerie warily. "I don't think that's quite my style."

"The color matches your toenails," her sister pointed out.

"Which is proof that I've ventured far enough out of my comfort zone for today."

"I think Jordyn's right," Tristyn said. "You need to make a statement. Be bold. Be sexy."

"Who am I making a statement to?"

"Yourself," Jordyn said. "You're the only one who matters."

"I'm more of a white lace kind of girl," she told them.

"Because you like white lace or because Rob liked you in white lace?" Tristyn challenged.

Realizing that the answer to her sister's question was the latter, Lauryn impulsively grabbed the hanger from Jordyn's hand. "You're right—just because I've never worn purple satin doesn't mean that I shouldn't try it."

Tristyn handed her a red lace set. "Try this one, too."

After more shopping and dinner at Valentino's, Jordyn went home to her husband, but Tristyn convinced Lauryn—who wasn't in any hurry to go back to her empty house because the kids were spending the night with their grandparents—to go to Marg & Rita's for a drink. They arrived as another group was leaving and immediately snagged the just-vacated table by the bar.

Lauryn was sipping her second icy drink when Tristyn bobbled her own glass, nearly sloshing its contents over the rim.

"Ohmygod—he's here."

Lauryn glanced over her shoulder. "Who's here?"

Her sister sighed dreamily. "Hashtag yummy muscles."

She blinked. "Who?"

"We really need to get you on Twitter," Tristyn said, which didn't answer Lauryn's question at all. "Now he's at the bar."

She shifted her gaze, but there were so many people crowded around that area she still had no idea who was the focus of her sister's attention.

"Chatting with the fake blonde in the red dress," Tristyn told her.

She found the blonde in the red dress more easily and nodded in agreement with her sister's description. "Definitely fake."

Tristyn sighed. "Focus on the man."

Lauryn's gaze shifted again—and her heart actually skipped a beat when her gaze fell on Ryder Wallace.

"You *have* to introduce me. Please," her sister implored.

"You'll meet him on Monday," Lauryn reminded her.

Tristyn wiggled her eyebrows suggestively. "I want to meet him tonight and have breakfast with him in the morning."

She shook her head. "When are you going to realize that you spend so much time ogling other men because you don't want to admit that you have the hots for your boss?"

"Eww," Tristyn said. "My boss is our cousin."

"I was referring to the *other* half of Garrett-Slater Racing," she noted dryly.

"Josh Slater is *not* my boss," her sister said. "And I most assuredly do *not* have the hots for him."

Lauryn shrugged. "Go ahead—continue to live in denial."

Tristyn seemed happy enough to do that—and even happier still a minute later when she reached across the table to grab Lauryn's hand. "He's coming this way."

And only a few seconds later, he was standing beside their table.

Lauryn sighed, wondering how she'd gone so long without knowing who he was, and now it seemed that every time she turned around he was there. *"Ryder to the Rescue."*

She didn't know she'd spoken the words aloud until his lips curved.

"Actually, my last name is Wallace," he reminded her. "The 'to the Rescue' part is just for the show."

"I'm Tristyn," her sister said, offering her hand and a big smile. "And a huge fan of your show."

"It's a pleasure to meet you," he said, taking the proffered hand. "And this is my buddy, Dalton."

Lauryn hadn't even noticed the other man with Ryder, which proved she was as pathetic as her sister—only a little less obvious about it.

"Would it be all right if we joined you?" Ryder asked.

It would be rude to refuse when they were two people sitting at a table for four and there were no empty tables, but Lauryn was less interested in common courtesy than she was in self-preservation. The more time she spent in Ryder's company the more aware she was of him, and she definitely did not need to be crushing on the man who would be renovating her kitchen.

"Actually, you can have this table," she said. "We were just on our way out."

"No, we weren't," her sister immediately denied. "And yes, you can join us."

Ryder took the chair beside Lauryn; Dalton sat beside Tristyn. Although she suspected that her sister was a little disappointed by the seating arrangement, she didn't show it. She immediately started chatting with Ryder's friend—

who was, Lauryn finally noticed, almost as well-built and good-looking as America's Hottest Handyman.

"So what are you doing here?" she asked Ryder. "I would have thought Bar Down was more your style."

"And you'd be right," he confirmed. "But it was closed for a private party tonight."

She lifted her glass to her lips, frowning when she discovered it was empty. Before she could protest, Ryder had snagged the waitress to order another round of drinks for the table.

"We really should be going," Lauryn said, kicking her sister under the table. "It's getting late and—"

"And Kylie and Zachary are spending the night with their grandparents," Tristyn interjected.

Dalton seemed surprised by the revelation. "You have kids?"

Lauryn nodded. "Two of them."

"Husband?" he prompted.

"Not anymore."

"Hallelujah to that," Tristyn said, lifting her glass.

"My sister wasn't a fan," Lauryn noted dryly.

"What about you?" Tristyn asked Dalton. "Wife? Kids?"

He shook his head firmly. "Absolutely no entanglements."

"Good to know," Tristyn said, with a smile that conveyed a lot more than her words.

Which baffled Lauryn, because her sister had been all about Ryder until he actually came over to their table.

Ryder shifted a little closer to Lauryn to make room for the waitress who had returned with their drinks. As he did, his thigh brushed against hers, sending a jolt through her veins. Dalton took some bills out of his wallet as the waitress passed the drinks around. Lauryn immediately picked up her glass and took a long swallow of the icy liquid in a desperate attempt to cool her suddenly overheated body.

She pulled her phone out of her pocket, checked the screen.

"Expecting a call?" Ryder asked.

"Not really," she admitted. "But sometimes Kylie wakes up in the night looking for me. And this is Zachary's first sleepover because I was nursing him until a few weeks ago, when he started teething and it just got to be too painful to—" She broke off as heat flooded her cheeks. "And that was a little too much information."

Ryder just chuckled.

"I'm going to shut up now," she decided.

He touched her hand and she felt another jolt. "When I was four years old, my sister convinced me that I had a crack in my butt because the doctor dropped me when I was born."

She laughed at the outrageousness of the claim. "She did not."

"She did," he assured her solemnly. "And after that, every time I fell down, I was afraid parts of me would break off."

She shook her head, still smiling. "Why would you tell me something like that?"

"So that you wouldn't feel self-conscious about what you said. Now that you know something embarrassing about me, it levels the playing field."

"Do you always play fair?" she asked curiously.

His lips curved as he squeezed her hand gently before pulling his own away to pick up his beer. "Not always."

She wondered why it sounded more like a warning than an admission.

Chapter Six

After about an hour, Lauryn was forced to acknowledge that Ryder was more of a celebrity than she'd realized. During that time, several people—most of them female—had stopped by the table to say "hi" and tell him how much they enjoyed watching him on TV. Lauryn had assumed he would appreciate the attention, but she noticed that the ready smile on his lips wasn't reflected in his eyes. Apparently having legions of adoring fans could grow tiresome after a while.

Another frosty glass was set in front of her—was it her third? Fourth?—when she saw Dalton elbow his friend as the blonde in the red dress started toward their table. The woman looked a little unsteady and Ryder immediately murmured, "Excuse me," and rose to his feet to intercept her.

Lauryn sipped her drink as she watched him steer the woman toward the door and outside. He returned a few minutes later, giving a slight nod to his friend when he caught Dalton's eye.

"We've got to get an early start on a roofing job in the morning," Ryder said, winking at Lauryn, "so we're going to call it a night."

Dalton reluctantly pushed away from the table. "It was a pleasure meeting both of you."

Though his words encompassed both of them, Lauryn wasn't surprised that his gaze lingered on Tristyn. Her sister had that effect on a lot of men.

"Maybe we'll see you again," Tristyn said.

Dalton grinned. "I'm counting on it."

After Lauryn and Tristyn finished their drinks, they took a cab back to Lauryn's house. She lent her sister a pair of pajamas, and they crashed together in her bed like they'd done on many occasions in the past.

"If Jordyn was here, it would be just like old times," Tristyn noted.

"I don't remember my head spinning during those old times."

"It's the tequila," her sister told her.

"I don't drink tequila," Lauryn said. "Not since college."

"What do you think is in a margarita?"

She hadn't thought about it—she'd just enjoyed the sweet flavor of the pink lemonade margaritas. But thinking about it now elicited a regretful moan. "Tequila?"

"Yep."

Lauryn closed her eyes. "I guess I shouldn't drink margaritas, either."

She was almost drifting off to sleep before Tristyn spoke again. "Do you usually sleep in the middle now?"

"What?" She cracked open an eye to look at her sister.

"I assume you had a specific side of the bed when you shared it with Rob. I just wondered if you slept in the middle now that he's gone."

"We stopped sleeping together long before he walked out," she admitted. "He always claimed he fell asleep on the sofa, but I think that was just an excuse. In fact, I think the last time we had sex was when Zachary was conceived."

"You're kidding."

She shook her head, then grabbed the edge of the night table when the room spun around her. "He always blamed me for getting pregnant, as if it was something I'd done on my own."

Her sister was quiet for a minute, considering this information. "Did you ever suspect…that he was cheating on you?" she asked.

"After a few months without any physical connection, I started to wonder if maybe there was someone else," she admitted. "But I never asked, because I didn't want to know. Despite the obvious disconnect between us, I didn't want our marriage to be over."

"Have you had sex with anyone else since he left?"

"Of course not!"

"Why not?" Tristyn pressed.

"Because," she sputtered, so flustered by the question it took her a moment to come up with a more reasoned response. "I have two kids—I don't have the time or energy to even think about sex. And even if I had the time and the energy and a willing partner, I'm not exactly eager to bare a body that's not as tight or toned as it used to be."

"I saw you in that purple satin bra and undies—you look fabulous," Tristyn said loyally.

"And that's why you're my favorite sister tonight."

"I'm your favorite sister because I didn't make you come home alone to an empty house."

"I do appreciate that," Lauryn confirmed.

"Do you miss being married?" Tristyn asked curiously.

"No."

"Do you miss sex?"

Lauryn sighed. "I'm not even sure I remember what it is."

"We need to get you a Rabbit," her sister decided.

"Don't you think I have enough to keep me busy without adding a pet to the mix?"

Tristyn smirked. "I'm not referring to a furry bunny."

"What are you referring to?"

"A battery-operated adult toy."

She felt her cheeks burn. "I can't believe we're having this conversation."

"Sweetie, you've gone almost a year and a half without sex—that sure as heck can't be healthy."

"Things change when you have kids," Lauryn told her, a little defensively. "You don't have as much time for intimacy—or even the inclination."

"I don't believe it," Tristyn said. "If you're with the right guy, you find the time to be with him."

"Obviously, Rob wasn't the right guy," she said.

"Obviously," her sister agreed. "But he's been gone for almost nine months, and when I saw you with Ryder tonight, I got the distinct impression that he revs your engine."

Lauryn rolled her eyes. "You've been working in the racing industry for too long," she said, attempting to divert the conversation even as her thoughts drifted to Ryder and the completely unexpected—and unwelcome—tingles that danced over her skin whenever he was near.

"You're not denying it," Tristyn noted.

"I'm sure he revs the engine of every woman in America between the ages of seventeen and seventy."

"Undoubtedly," her sister agreed, then her tone became contemplative. "But while I've always found Ryder Wallace to be incredibly appealing, you're usually attracted to pretty boys."

"You think Rob was a pretty boy?"

"Just because I didn't like him doesn't mean I couldn't appreciate that he had a certain metrosexual appeal," Tristyn said. "Ryder Wallace is the complete opposite—a man's man. And the more I think about it, the more I think it might be interesting to stick around and watch the two of you together."

"We're not going to be together. He's going to renovate my kitchen and I'm going to keep the kids out of the way."

"That's disappointing."

"And anyway, he left the bar tonight with the blonde in the red dress."

"He walked out with her," Tristyn acknowledged. "But I don't think he went home with her."

"What makes you say that?"

"Because even as he was walking out the door, he was looking at you."

Lauryn squinted at her sister. "How many margaritas did you have?"

"He was looking at *you*," Tristyn said again. "And you were looking right back at him."

She sighed. "He is really nice to look at."

And with that thought and his image lingering in her mind, she finally drifted off to sleep.

Lauryn had never been much of a drinker. Even back in college, she rarely overindulged, and since becoming a mother, "rarely" became "never." She did enjoy the occasional glass of wine—sometimes even two, but the four cocktails she'd tossed back the night before were an unprecedented experience. And the banging inside her head the next morning confirmed it was an experience she could have lived without.

"What the hell?" Tristyn grumbled, her face buried in the pillow beside her.

Lauryn winced as her sister's words sliced through her skull like daggers. "Can you 'what the hell' a little more quietly, please?" she begged softly. "The pounding inside my head is punishment enough for last night."

"The pounding's not in your head," Tristyn told her. "I think it's on the roof."

Lauryn reluctantly pulled the covers off her face and pried open her eyelids to look at the ceiling, then frowned. "What the… Oh."

"Oh?" her sister prompted.

Throwing back the covers, she jumped out of bed, hurried down the stairs and out the front door. Heedless of the

damp grass beneath her bare feet, she ventured into the
middle of the lawn so that she could see the roof, holding up
a hand to shield her eyes from the piercing glare of daylight.

The sun was behind him, outlining his impressive phy-
sique: incredibly broad shoulders stretching out a forest
green T-shirt, strong arms tightly corded with muscle and
lightly dusted with gold hair, long powerful legs hugged
by faded denim.

Looking at him standing there, Lauryn's mouth actually
went dry. Or maybe that was a residual effect of the tequila.

"Good morning." he called down, when he saw her looking up at him.

Her response was much less amiable. "What the hell are
you doing on my roof, Ryder?"

Ryder knew he shouldn't stare, but the sight of Lauryn standing on the front lawn—her fists propped on hips
clad in a pair of silky boxer shorts, her sexily tousled hair
spilling over her shoulders and her green eyes blazing—
rendered him unable to do anything else. The top of her
head barely came up to his chin, but her shapely bare legs
seemed endless and the skimpy little tank top she wore over
the boxers hugged her feminine curves and made him wish
he could do the same.

His crew chief, always attuned to any potential problems, put down his nail gun to join Ryder at the edge of
the roof. Stan whistled under his breath. "Is that the home
owner?"

"That's Mrs. Schulte," Ryder confirmed.

Stan was quiet for a minute, taking in the situation—or
maybe just admiring the view.

"You won't have to worry about anyone showing up late
for this job," his crew chief assured him. "The guys will be
more than happy to work under her. Or over her. Or—" He

wisely swallowed the rest of his words when Ryder slid him a glance, then cleared his throat. "No disrespect intended."

He nodded. "Help Dalton finish up here with the water shield. I'll go see what Mrs. Schulte wants."

As he climbed down the ladder propped up at the side of the house, Lauryn headed to meet him. She made quite a picture striding across the grass, and he let his gaze skim over her again. Though he knew she couldn't see his eyes through the dark lenses of his sunglasses, he forced his gaze up to her face when she halted in front of him. "Is there a problem?" he asked.

"That depends on whether or not you consider a bunch of men banging on your roof at seven thirty in the morning a problem."

"I'm guessing we woke you up."

She shoved a wayward strand of dark hair away from her face. "Good guess."

"I'm sorry," he said. "There was no answer when I knocked and no vehicle in the driveway, so I assumed you were out."

"At seven thirty in the morning?"

He shrugged. "Or didn't come home."

"What do you mean—my van isn't here?" She glanced over her shoulder and discovered that there were two trucks—one bearing the Renovations by Ryder logo and the other advertising Dalton's Roofing—taking up the length of driveway. "Oh, right. Tristyn and I cabbed it back last night."

He tilted his head to study her more closely. "I'm guessing that was a good idea. Head hurt this morning?"

"Only because I woke up to someone banging on my roof," she told him.

"The tequila had nothing to do with it?" he challenged.

"The effects of the tequila would have worn off after a couple more hours of sleep," she said, her cheeks flushing.

"Then I'll apologize for waking you, but the forecast was for clear skies and Dalton had the weekend free. I thought you would appreciate getting the roof done as soon as possible."

"I do, of course," she agreed. "I just didn't realize it would be this soon."

"We actually started yesterday," he told her. "Tearing off the old shingles and replacing the wet plywood. You didn't see the Dumpster at the side of the house?"

"No, I didn't," she admitted as her sister—fully clothed—crossed the lawn toward them.

"And when we left Marg & Rita's last night, I told you it was because we needed to get an early start today."

She vaguely remembered him saying something about a roofing job, but she hadn't realized he'd been referring to her roof. "Will you be finished today?" Lauryn asked.

He glanced up at the clear sky. "I can't imagine why not."

"Perhaps because the men who are supposed to be working are all focused on your conversation," Tristyn suggested.

He shifted his gaze to his buddies, who were staring down from the roof without any pretense of working. He shook his head, but he knew he really couldn't blame them. "I don't think they're as interested in any conversation as they are in your sister's underwear."

Lauryn gasped softly and immediately folded her arms over her chest. The action succeeded in covering up her puckered nipples but also pushed up her breasts, enhancing the cleavage displayed by the low neckline of her tank.

"This isn't my underwear," she denied hotly.

"Then what is it?" he asked.

"My pajamas."

"Semantics," her sister said, handing her a robe. "And irrelevant when the curve of your butt cheeks is visible for the workmen and all of your neighbors to see."

Lauryn shoved her arms into the sleeves of the garment and yanked the belt around her waist, glaring at Ryder the whole time. "This is *your* fault."

He lifted a brow. "How is it my fault?"

"You were making so much noise on the roof I didn't stop to think about what I was wearing."

"Or not wearing," her sister interjected.

Ryder fought against the smile that wanted to curve his lips in response to the words that perfectly echoed his own thoughts. Of course, Tristyn could afford to tease Lauryn because she was wearing actual clothes.

The color in Lauryn's cheeks deepened in response to the teasing. "You remember my sister, Tristyn?"

He nodded. "I apologize for the wake-up call."

"Please don't," she said, her eyes sparkling with humor. "I'm happy to tell everyone I know that I was awakened by America's Hottest Handyman."

He winced. "I'd rather you didn't."

"While you two conduct your meeting of the Ryder Wallace Fan Club, I'm going to go drown myself in the shower," Lauryn told them.

"There's coffee on in the kitchen," Tristyn said.

Lauryn nodded as she headed back toward the house.

"Coffee?" Ryder echoed hopefully.

"Come on in," she invited.

He followed her through the front door, down the short, wide hallway to the kitchen, where the scent of the fresh brew teased his nostrils.

Tristyn, obviously at home in her sister's kitchen, took down two mugs from the cupboard and filled them from the carafe. "Cream or sugar?" she asked him.

"Sugar, please."

She retrieved the bowl and a spoon and set them on the counter. She drank her own black—and watched him so intently he began to feel as if he was in *his* pajamas.

"Is something wrong?" he finally asked.

"Not at all," she assured him. "The dim lighting in the bar didn't really do you justice, and I was just appreciating the fact that you're even better looking in person than on TV."

"Thank you," he said cautiously.

"Don't worry—I'm not hitting on you. Not that I wouldn't be tempted, under other circumstances," she admitted. "But even a little foggy from the tequila last night, I could see the sparks between you and Lauryn. Which is why I was so puzzled when you left with the clingy blonde in the clingier red dress."

"I think the tequila had more of an effect than you realized," he told her, ignoring her comment about the blonde.

"Are you denying that there's a certain…chemistry… between you and my sister?"

"I think you're misinterpreting friction as attraction," he told her. "She's not at all looking forward to her home being invaded by me and my crew."

"I know," she admitted.

"But you didn't anticipate that when you forged her name on an application?"

"I suspected that she might have some objections," Tristyn acknowledged. "But when we sent in the application, we didn't really think it would be chosen. Not out of the hundreds you must have received."

"Actually, we got close to a thousand," he told her.

"And somehow, out of all of those, you selected Lauryn's application," she mused.

"You mean *your* application."

She chose to ignore the clarification. "It kind of makes me think that fate had a hand in your selection."

"Fate?" he echoed dubiously.

"I was a skeptic, too," she told him. "But the way the stars aligned for my other sister and her husband last year,

I'm starting to believe some things might be written in the heavens."

"And that excuses you signing your sister's name?"

"Sometimes the end does justify the means. And Lauryn deserves this. She *needs* this. After everything she's been through this past year…and years before."

He didn't ask. Though Ryder was undeniably curious about Lauryn's history, it wasn't really any of his business.

"So how did you get her to agree to it?" Tristyn asked him.

"I had a little help from Mother Nature," he admitted.

"The leaky roof?" she guessed.

He nodded. "The rain was coming into Kylie's bedroom."

"If it had been her own bedroom, she would have put out buckets and lived with it as long as she had to," Tristyn said. "If you've been given a tour of the house, you probably noticed that Kylie's and Zachary's rooms are the only ones that have been updated in forty years."

"I noticed," he confirmed.

"Rob made her so many promises…" Tristyn trailed off, shaking her head. "He agreed to everything she wanted when they were first married—and did absolutely nothing."

"You obviously weren't a fan."

"No," she admitted. "I tried to like him, because Lauryn loved him, but I couldn't get beyond reluctant tolerance."

"He couldn't have been that bad if your sister stayed with him for so long," Ryder surmised.

"Lauryn doesn't like to fail at anything. Once she spoke her vows, she was determined to do everything in her power to make the marriage work. But a relationship takes two people, and Rob wasn't half as committed as she was."

Maybe he should have felt guilty that he was talking to Lauryn's sister about her, but he wasn't interrogating her—they were just having a conversation. And he suspected that Tristyn wouldn't tell him anything she didn't want him to know.

Especially not with Lauryn's footsteps coming down the stairs.

"Feel better?" Tristyn asked when her sister entered the kitchen.

"Much." Lauryn poured herself a mug of coffee, added a splash of milk and took a long sip.

"You found your clothes," Ryder noted. "I'm disappointed."

She narrowed her gaze. "Aren't you supposed to be working on the roof?"

"Everything's under control," he assured her.

"Where's the camera crew?" Tristyn asked. "There doesn't seem to be anyone filming what you're doing today."

"Lucky for your sister," he teased.

Now that the shower had washed away the tequila-induced cobwebs, Lauryn could admit that her decision to storm outside and confront Ryder had been both impulsive and regrettable. Unfortunately, there was no way to undo what she had done, so she attempted to appeal to his sense of decency instead. "Can we *please* just forget about this morning?"

"I don't think so," he said. "But I can stop talking about your underwear, if it makes you uncomfortable."

"I was wearing *pajamas*," she said through gritted teeth.

"The camera crew?" Tristyn prompted again, in an obvious attempt to redirect the conversation.

"They don't usually work weekends and they don't work at all without a signed contract." He slid an envelope across the table. "The terms have been revised, per our previous discussion. Now we just need your signature."

"If you don't have a contract, why are you here?" Tristyn asked.

"Because I wanted to get the roof done before it rained again. Thankfully, it's in pretty good shape." He turned his attention back to Lauryn. "Dalton said the biggest problem was some patchwork that was done around the chimney without replacing the flashing—that's why the water was getting into your attic and then Kylie's bedroom from there.

"And speaking of the attic," he continued, "do you mind if I take another look up there to ensure everything's drying out?"

"Of course not," she said. Then Lauryn thought about the fact that the attic access was in her bedroom—and the new lingerie her sisters had bought for her was on top of her dresser. "But why don't you have another cup of coffee first?"

"Why?" he asked, obviously having picked up on something in her tone.

"Because…I can't remember if I made my bed," she improvised, setting down her mug and heading back to the stairs.

"I've seen unmade beds before," he assured her.

"Just give me a minute," she said, hurrying up to her bedroom. She swept the lingerie off the dresser and into the top drawer. And then, because her bed was unmade, she took a minute to pull up the sheets and comforter.

Ryder stepped into the room just as she was tying back the curtains. Sunlight spilled through the window, illuminating a scrap of red fabric on the floor in front of the dresser.

He bent down and picked it up.

She suspected that her face burned a brighter shade of crimson than the thong dangling from Ryder's finger.

"As much as I liked your pajamas," he said, "I like your underwear even more."

Chapter Seven

Lauryn snatched the lacy fabric out of his hand and stuffed it into the drawer. "You wanted to look in the attic," she reminded him.

"I did," he agreed, intrigued by the color in her cheeks. "But now I'm much more interested in the goodies you have in that dresser."

"Could you *please* focus on the reason you're here?"

"I can multitask," he assured her, reaching up to lower the staircase. "As for the reason I'm here…did you ever consider that this room could use a makeover?"

"Never," she told him.

"That was sarcasm, right?"

"No, I think the blue-and-green-plaid wallpaper really works with the chocolate comforter and pink accents."

"That was definitely sarcasm," he noted.

She looked around the room, shrugged. "I was going to tear it down," she admitted. "Whoever owned the house before we bought it obviously loved bold-patterned wallpaper, because it was *everywhere*. But after the hassle of scraping ugly roosters off Kylie's walls, I decided I could live with this plaid a little while longer."

"There were roosters in Kylie's room?"

"And flocked velvet flowers on a black background in what is now Zachary's room," she told him.

"I guess there's no accounting for taste," he acknowledged.

"And while I obviously want to get rid of this plaid at some point in time, it's not something I'm anxious to tackle with two kids underfoot. And, truthfully, I've become so accustomed to it that I don't even see it anymore." She shrugged. "And since nobody else usually sees it, I don't worry about it."

He figured he'd have to be blind not to see the wallpaper, but he chose to focus on the first part of her statement, instead. "The kids aren't here now, and I'd be happy to help you strip." He grinned. "The wallpaper, I mean."

"While I appreciate the offer," she said, in a tone that sounded less than appreciative, "I don't have time today. I have to be at The Locker Room before noon."

"Zumba class?" he guessed, because she didn't look like the type to pump iron.

"What?"

"Is that what you do at the gym?" He'd dated a Zumba instructor a few months previously and now had a keen appreciation for the benefits of aerobic dance on the female body.

She smiled as she shook her head. "I'm not going to work out but to work. The Locker Room is my business."

"I thought you worked at Garrett Furniture."

"Not since my ex left me his failing sporting goods store in exchange for all of the money in our joint bank accounts."

"Your husband really was a prince, wasn't he?"

"There was a time when I thought he was," she admitted. "And that was my mistake."

While her tone was matter-of-fact, her eyes were filled with so much sadness he was immediately contrite. "I'm sorry."

"You were on your way up to the attic," she reminded him again, a clear indication that their conversation was at an end.

He nodded and started up the stairs, but while he was inspecting the space, his mind was only half on the task. Or maybe only a third. Because another part of him was wanting to soothe her obvious heartache, and another part was wanting to see her in the lacy red thong that he'd found on the floor of her bedroom.

Until she'd stormed outside in her pajamas earlier that morning, he hadn't given a single thought to her underwear. And why would he? He was a contractor, she was his client and he'd never before crossed that line. Even when a client had made it clear that she'd be interested in playing with his tools, he'd never been tempted. Until now.

But he could—and would—resist the temptation. Because a divorcée with two small children had *complication* written all over her, and he preferred simple relationships. And red lace. Yeah, he really liked red lace. And soft curves and fragrant skin and—

Damn, her sister was right. There was some definite chemistry there. And while he was both attracted and intrigued, he knew that the best thing he could do was keep his distance from the sexy single mom. Because she was all about family, and he didn't have the first clue what it meant to be part of one.

He pushed her out of his mind and returned his attention to the ceiling. He was able to confirm that everything was drying out nicely and there were no other problem areas. There were some boxes piled in one corner, many of them marked "Christmas decorations" and several others indicating Kylie's first birthday, Kylie's baby clothes, Kylie's art and crafts. There were no less than half a dozen boxes for a child who wasn't even four years old. Obviously, Lauryn was a doting and sentimental mother—or a hopeless pack rat. His own mother had been neither—she'd never even put her children's artwork on the refrigerator, and when their nanny had done so, she'd complained about the clutter.

He shook off the memories and the melancholy, gathered the pots that he'd set out a few days earlier to collect the leaking water and headed back downstairs.

He could hear Lauryn talking before he entered the kitchen. Since it sounded like a one-sided conversation, he guessed that she was on the phone. He hesitated in the hallway, not wanting to interrupt but not wanting to eavesdrop, either.

"You're a sweetie, Jackson." Those brief words alleviated his reluctance to listen in on her conversation. "I don't know a lot of lawyers who would take time out of their Sunday mornings to help out a nonpaying client."

Of course, Ryder couldn't hear what Jackson said after that, but his response made Lauryn chuckle—and made Ryder wonder about her relationship with the lawyer.

"True," she agreed. "Give my love to Kelly and the kids."

Ryder waited until she'd set down the phone before he stepped into the kitchen. "Jackson?" he queried.

"My cousin," she explained. "He's an attorney in upstate New York."

He was inexplicably relieved by her explanation and glanced at the papers spread out on the table, with notes penciled in the margins. "Do you have questions about the contract?"

"Not now," she said. "But I learned the hard way not to sign anything unless and until I understand every word."

The slight edge to her tone suggested there was a story there—no doubt involving the ex-husband in some way—but he reminded himself that he would be doing them both a favor by keeping their relationship strictly business. No confidences or confessions required.

"And you're still not thrilled about doing the show," he guessed.

"No, but I won't renege on our agreement," she promised.

"Look on the bright side," he suggested.

"There's a bright side?" she asked, sounding skeptical.

"You can finally say goodbye to this ugly brown linoleum."

Lauryn managed a tight smile as she picked up her pen

and turned to the final page, scrawling her name on the signature line without further hesitation.

Because he was right. She'd hated that floor for more than six years—although much like the plaid wallpaper in her bedroom, she'd become so accustomed to the cracked vinyl that she barely noticed it anymore. And even if Kylie had taken her first steps on that linoleum, the memories wouldn't be torn away along with the flooring. And maybe Zachary would take his first steps in the new kitchen.

Still, as she added her signature to the second copy of the contract, she couldn't help feeling that she'd sold out. Not that she really had a choice. Whether or not the producers of *Ryder to the Rescue* would really take legal action against Tristyn and Jordyn for falsifying the application, she wasn't willing to take the chance of causing any negative publicity for her family. And with the financial difficulties of The Locker Room hanging over her head, she knew there wasn't going to be any extra money for home improvements anytime soon, not to mention the new roof that was—thank you, Ryder Wallace—already being installed.

"Where'd your sister go?" he asked her now.

"My cousin Daniel picked her up to take her to Charlotte for the race today." She slid the signed papers back into the envelope and handed it to Ryder. "So it all starts tomorrow?"

He nodded. "We'll be here by eight—I hope that's not too early."

"That's fine." She checked her purse for the essentials—wallet, keys, cell phone. "Are we done here now? Because I need to call a cab so that I can pick up my van."

"I can give you a ride."

"Oh." While she appreciated his willingness to help her out, she knew that she should decline his offer. To another woman, the butterflies that fluttered in her tummy whenever he was near might indicate anticipation, but to

Lauryn they were a warning sign—and one that she intended to heed. Which meant that she needed to set very clear boundaries for a strictly professional relationship with Ryder Wallace. "Thanks, but I don't want to take you away from your work."

"It's not a problem," he insisted. "And it will give us a chance to talk about your ideas for the kitchen."

Which sounded perfectly reasonable and definitely within the boundaries of their working relationship. And it would save her the cost of cab fare. "That would be great—thanks."

After Ryder dropped Lauryn off at her van and watched her drive away, he made a quick detour to the grocery store, then stopped by the condo where his sister now lived with her husband and new baby.

"This is a nice surprise," Avery said, opening the door to let him in. "But definitely a surprise."

"I wanted to see how my beautiful niece is doing."

"What about your beautiful sister?"

He grinned and kissed her cheek. "Her, too, of course. In fact, I brought her a present," he said, handing Avery the tub of ice cream he'd picked up.

She eyed the gift in her hand warily. "Why did you bring me ice cream?"

He frowned at her unexpected response. "It's cookies 'n' cream—isn't that your favorite?"

"It is," she confirmed with a sigh. "But I just had a baby three weeks ago and I've still got fourteen pounds to lose."

He reached for the container that she was eyeing with equal parts longing and suspicion. "Fine—I'll take it home with me."

She hugged the tub to her chest and slapped at his hand. "No, you won't. You can't come in here waving ice cream around and then take it away."

"Can I trade it for a cup of coffee?" he asked.

"That sounds reasonable," she decided.

He followed her to the kitchen, marveling over how much her life had changed this year. As much as Avery loved babies, she'd had deep-seated doubts about her ability to be a good mother—an understandable consequence of their dysfunctional upbringing.

But from the minute she learned of her pregnancy, she'd done everything possible to be the best mother that she could be. Ryder was happy for his sister because she was happy, but that didn't mean he wanted the same thing for himself. He liked being single and couldn't imagine that he'd ever want to complicate his life with marriage and kids.

"There she is," he said softly, moving toward the kitchen island where his niece was sleeping, securely buckled into some kind of baby seat. "Is it possible that she gets cuter every time I see her?"

"Of course. And I say that with absolutely no bias whatsoever," Avery told him.

He shifted his attention to her. "I had some reservations when you first told me about your pregnancy—and especially when you told me the father was a doctor," he admitted. "But looking at you now...I honestly don't think I've ever seen you look happier or more content."

"I never thought I could be this happy," she admitted, sliding a mug of coffee across the table to him. "I lucked out with Justin—he's a wonderful husband and father. And Vanessa, fingers crossed, is a very good baby."

"Of course, she is. She's perfect."

Avery rolled her eyes. "So tell me what's happening with you."

"We're finally ready to start the last Room Rescue."

"You say that as if there was a delay."

"It turns out the home owner wasn't thrilled by the idea of camera crews on her property," he confided, lifting the mug to his lips to sip the coffee she'd already sweetened for him.

"She didn't think about that before she filled out the application?" his sister asked, sounding surprised.

"Well, that's another story," he said, then realized she might be able to fill in some of the missing details. "How well do you know Justin's cousin, Lauryn?"

"Not well," she said. "And not because of Justin. I delivered her baby."

"Zachary."

Her brows lifted at his use of the baby's name. "How do you—oh," she realized. "Lauryn is the third winner of your contest?"

He nodded.

"It's starting to make sense now," she said. "From the little that Justin has said, she's an intensely private person—not the type to compete for a spot on a television program."

"You're right," he confirmed, and told her about Lauryn's sisters submitting the application on her behalf.

"How did you end up picking her application, anyway?"

"I thought she was married," he admitted. "In addition to the mention of a husband, there was a notable absence of nude photos and explicit propositions."

She chuckled at that. "If you'd chosen an application with nude photos, you'd be facing a lot less resistance right now."

"I'd rather deal with resistance than sexual harassment." A slight movement caught the corner of his eye and he turned to see Vanessa lifting her arms up, her little hands clenched into fists, her tiny rosebud mouth opening in a yawn. "Hey, look who's waking up. And smiling at me."

"It's gas," Avery said, rolling her eyes.

"It is *not*," he denied. "She knows her favorite uncle when she's looking at him."

"Justin has two brothers who might want to challenge that title."

"But they're not here right now and I am," he said, unfastening the plastic buckle around the baby's belly and lifting her from her seat.

"She's going to be hungry," Avery said. "Every three hours like clockwork."

"Well, she's not fussing right now," he noted, tucking her into the crook of his arm. "But maybe she should eat—she still doesn't weight half as much as my tool belt."

"She's gained over a pound since we brought her home from the hospital."

"That hardly makes her a heavyweight."

"Dr. Kertz is pleased with her progress," she assured him.

"What does he think of that flower growing out of her head?" he asked, studying the fabric daisy with apparent concern.

"It's a headband," she said. "She doesn't have a lot of hair yet, and I want people to know that she's a girl."

He looked around the condo. "What people? And isn't the pink outfit enough of a clue?"

She shrugged. "Justin came home with all of these little accessories for her—headbands and frilly socks—and I know he likes to see her wearing them."

"Speaking of your husband, this is the first time I've been here and not found him hovering over both of you."

"He's at the hospital today."

"Are you itching to get back?" he wondered.

"I thought I would be," she admitted. "But I'm going to take some time, then Justin and I want to coordinate our schedules so that one of us is with Vanessa as much as possible."

"Not planning on hiring a nanny?"

"Not ruling it out," she acknowledged. "But if we did, it would only be for a few hours a day—I have no intention of paying someone else to raise my child."

"You're already a better mother than ours ever was," Ryder told her.

"Daddyhood looks like it would fit you pretty well, too," she noted.

He immediately shook his head and shoved the baby at his sister. "No way. I'm not ready to be domesticated."

But then he remembered the way Kylie had looked at him, with absolute trust in her big blue eyes. And the way he'd felt, like he was a superhero, when she'd wrapped her arms around him. And he considered that being a daddy—under the right circumstances and in the distant future—might not be so bad.

"Since you mentioned our mother," Avery began, settling the baby against her shoulder.

"Just a slip of the tongue," he assured her.

"Well, she's coming to town next weekend to meet her granddaughter."

"Really?"

"I was as surprised as you are," she admitted. "And I'm not entirely convinced that her plans won't change between now and then, but if they don't...could you pick her up at the airport?"

"Can't she take a cab?"

"Come on, Ryder—she's our mother."

"I'm still not entirely convinced," he said. "When I visited her lab in Atlanta, I got a much warmer feeling from one of the test tubes."

"Ha-ha." But he could tell his sister wasn't amused.

He sighed. "When does her flight get in?"

"I'll text the details to you as soon as they're confirmed," she told him. "Thank you."

"You know I can't say 'no' to you, but if you're expecting a happy family reunion next weekend, you're going to be disappointed."

"I was thinking birthday party rather than reunion," she admitted.

"No way," he said firmly.

"But I always make dinner for you on your birthday."

"That was before you had a husband and a baby to take care of."

"As surprising as it may seem, neither getting married nor giving birth stripped me of my ability to cook."

"I'm sure that's true," he said. "But, as it turns out, I already have plans for dinner on my birthday."

Her eyes narrowed. "Why don't I believe you?"

"Apparently you're cynical and untrusting—you should work on that."

His sister was undeterred. "Who are these plans with?"

"You know I don't kiss and tell."

"Well, don't be kissing my husband's cousin," she said.

He frowned, uncomfortable with his sister's uncanny ability to read his thoughts and feelings. "Where did *that* come from?"

"I've known you forever," she reminded him. "So I know that what you don't say is often more telling than what you do."

"Well, you're way off base this time," he told her.

"I hope I am," she said. "But you've never walked away from anything that needed to be fixed."

"Houses," he clarified. "I fix houses."

"And while you're renovating Lauryn's kitchen, you'll likely be spending a fair amount of time with her."

"I've lost count of the number of kitchen renos I've done," he told her. "There's no cause for concern on this one."

"Those Garretts have a way of sneaking into your heart when you least expect it," she warned.

"You don't have to worry—single moms aren't my type," he assured her.

"And doctors weren't mine," she said pointedly.

Chapter Eight

Lauryn was on her way back downstairs after tucking Kylie into bed Sunday night when she saw headlights turn into the driveway. As the vehicle drew closer to the house, she recognized it as Jordyn's hatchback.

She didn't know why her sister had stopped by, but she was grateful for any distraction from thoughts of the upcoming renovation that had plagued her throughout the day. She only hoped it was the inevitable mess and presence of the construction crews that worried her, rather than the man who was the center of the show.

"You're eleven hours early," she said, meeting her sister at the door.

"I didn't forget about the taping tomorrow," Jordyn assured her. "But I wanted to get this to you tonight."

"What's this?" she asked, taking the proffered folder.

"A business proposal." Jordyn kicked off her shoes and headed down the hall.

As her sister helped herself to a can of soda from the fridge, Lauryn settled at the table and opened the cover of the folder. She quickly scanned the contents and was already shaking her head before she got to the bottom of the first page. "I can't let you invest in the business."

"Why not?"

"Because it's too risky. The Locker Room hasn't been in the black for the past three years."

"Because it's been poorly inventoried, overstaffed and

mismanaged," her sister pointed out, pouring the soda into a glass.

"All of that's true," she agreed. "And there's no guarantee that I can turn it around."

"You're a Garrett," Jordyn reminded her, conveniently ignoring the fact that Lauryn's surname had been Schulte for more than six years. And while Lauryn had been tempted to take back "Garrett" when her husband walked out, she'd decided to keep "Schulte" for the sake of her kids.

"And with two more Garretts on board—and countless others waiting in the wings to offer advice and expertise you may not want or need—I don't see any other possible scenario," Jordyn continued.

Lauryn couldn't help but smile at that, but still she hesitated to take what her sisters were offering. She'd made mistakes in her life and she was paying for them—she didn't want her sisters to pay, too. The amount of money that Rob had dumped into the store—and lost—was staggering to her, and she didn't know if it was even possible to get out of the mountain of debt he'd left behind. "I appreciate what you're trying to do, but—"

"No buts," Jordyn said, sitting across from her. "Tristyn and I are both committed to this."

"When did you come up with this plan? I only told you about the situation at breakfast yesterday."

"She stopped by the house on her way to Charlotte this morning. Interestingly enough, we were both already thinking along the same lines."

"Did you talk to Marco about this?" she asked, aware that her sister's husband had a lot invested in his own business ventures.

"Of course, I did. And he fully supports what we're doing."

"Because he hasn't seen the books," Lauryn said, only half joking.

"Because he knows that I wouldn't be doing this if I didn't have complete faith in you," her sister clarified.

Still, Lauryn hesitated.

"Stop being stubborn," Jordyn told her. "You don't have to do everything on your own."

"I know. I just don't want to count on other people to clean up my messes."

"This wasn't your mess."

"Wasn't it?" Lauryn challenged.

"Your only mistake was marrying a man who didn't deserve you," her sister insisted.

Lauryn pulled the glass across the table and picked it up for a sip. "And I'm in the financial mess I'm in now because I married him."

"Now you're being stupid as well as stubborn," Jordyn said. "And if you don't take the deal that we're offering, we'll tell Dad."

She choked on the soda. "Are we in grade school? If I don't do what you want, you're going to run and tell Daddy?"

"Yep." Jordyn was unapologetic as she took her drink back. "And you know what he'll do—he'll buy the building, even the whole block, if necessary."

Lauryn didn't doubt that it was true. It was one of the reasons she hadn't shared any of the details of the situation with her parents.

"The bank wouldn't give me any money." She felt compelled to point that out to her sister. "Doesn't that tell you something about the state of the business?"

"It only tells me that I need to switch banks—and you probably should, too."

Lauryn thumbed through the clearly drafted agreement again. Jordyn took a pen out of her pocket and set it down on top of the papers.

"I'm not signing anything without talking to my lawyer," she said, attempting to stall her sister.

"Your lawyer drafted the agreement," Jordyn told her.

"He did?"

"Do you think we'd trust anyone but Jackson with this?"

Of course not. And there wasn't anyone Lauryn trusted more than her sisters. This time when Jordyn nudged the pen toward her, Lauryn picked it up and signed her name.

Lauryn was expecting Ryder and his crew when they showed up at eight o'clock the next morning, but that didn't mean she was any more comfortable about the whole scenario. She hovered in the background as the camera operators and AV techs walked through the hall and the kitchen, figuring out where to set up lights and microphones and stationary cameras. By nine, they were ready to begin.

"This is our home owner, Lauryn Schulte, who lives in this 1972 traditional Foursquare with her children."

The show's director, Owen Diercks, had wanted the kids on camera. "Our viewers love kids," he told Lauryn. But Kylie, although already a fan of Ryder, was less certain about all of the other people who had invaded her home, and Lauryn wasn't prepared to force her outside of her comfort zone. As a result, after seeing her daughter safely onto the school bus, she'd opted for Zachary to remain off screen, too, under the watchful eyes of Jordyn and Tristyn.

"How long have you lived here, Lauryn?" Ryder asked her.

"A little more than six years now."

"And how long have you been planning to renovate?"

"A little more than six years," she admitted. "When we bought the house, the plan was to update the kitchen as soon as possible."

"Obviously, that plan changed."

"My husband had his own business, so he didn't have the time to do the renovations we wanted to do.

"In the beginning, I was employed full-time outside of

the home, too. Then, after our daughter was born, I continued to work part-time in retail as well as take care of her."

"And now you have two children?" Ryder prompted.

She nodded. "Kylie's three and a half and Zachary is seven months."

"So when you heard about the Room Rescue contest, did you decide that would be the perfect opportunity to get a new kitchen?"

"Well, that's not quite how it happened," she admitted. "In fact, I didn't even know about the contest—it was my sisters who filled out the application on my behalf."

"How did you feel when you found out what they'd done?" he prompted.

"I was embarrassed that they had believed it was necessary to bring in outside help to complete the renovation—and because they were right. I've hated this kitchen for more than six years. I certainly didn't want to go on TV and show it off to your viewers."

"Well, let's bring in your sisters now so that they can tell their side of the story."

After Tristyn and Jordyn were introduced, they explained their decision to fill out an application on Lauryn's behalf—and expressed their excitement that the application had actually been chosen by Ryder for inclusion in the program.

"At this point, I would usually introduce you to Monica Snyder, our design expert," Ryder said, speaking to the viewers as much as to Lauryn. "It's her job to meet with the home owners, to determine what changes they consider essential and what other features they would like to add to the room under renovation, then decide how to make it happen within the allotted budget.

"But Monica spent the weekend mountain biking at Warrior Creek, where she took an unfortunate spill and broke her leg."

"Oh, my goodness," Lauryn said, her concern immediate and genuine. "Is she going to be okay?"

Ryder nodded. "She's going to be fine, but she's also going to be in the hospital for a few days and laid up for several weeks after that."

"So who's going to design my kitchen?" Lauryn asked, feeling slightly panicked.

"You are," he told her. Then he dropped an enormous binder on the table in front of her. "With a little assistance from what Monica refers to as her planning bible."

"I think I'm going to need a lot of assistance."

"Haven't you been thinking about this kitchen renovation since you bought the house?"

She nodded. "I must have redesigned this room a dozen times in my mind over the years, but I never made any final decisions. Probably because I wasn't sure this renovation was ever going to happen."

"It's going to happen now," Ryder assured her.

And, surrounded by the cameras and his crew, she was finally starting to believe it.

The morning taping kept Lauryn tied up longer than she'd expected, and it was after noon before she was able to make her escape. Then she had to meet Kylie's bus, load both of the kids into the van and head over to her parents' house so that Susan could watch them while Lauryn relieved Bree, one of only two part-time employees at The Locker Room.

Thankfully, she didn't have to worry about feeding Kylie and Zachary. She'd called her mother before she left home to let her know they were going to be hungry, and Susan had lunch ready when they arrived—including a sandwich for Lauryn to take with her. *Thank goodness for my family*, she thought to herself as she kissed Kylie and Zachary, then gave her mom a quick hug. She honestly didn't know how she would've have made it through the past nine months without them.

Mondays tended to be quiet at the store. Not that The Locker Room did a brisk business any day of the week, but on Mondays, in particular, the hours seemed to drag. With few customers to tend to, Lauryn spent her time tidying up displays and re-shelving misplaced merchandise. When the bell over the door rang, she turned toward the front of the store with a ready smile on her face.

The smile froze when she recognized the man who walked through the door.

"Ryder."

"Hello, Lauryn."

"Is there something I can help you find?" she asked, pretending he was just another customer.

"Actually, I was looking for you," he said. But he took a minute to glance around the store. "You've recently done some work in here."

"A few cosmetic touches to refresh the store's image."

"I like the color."

"Jordyn has a good eye for that kind of thing."

"An important quality in an artist, I would think."

She seemed surprised that he'd remembered the detail that she'd dropped into a casual conversation several days earlier, but Ryder had always believed that good customer service started with paying attention to his clients and listening to what they wanted—which was why he was here.

"We need to decide on a cabinet style and color as soon as possible. My supplier is expecting a big order for a new development in the north end, and we want to get yours in ahead of that or the original four- to six-week time frame could end up being ten to twelve."

"Then I guess I'd better decide on my cabinets."

"Based on what seemed to catch your eye when you were looking through Monica's book, I've narrowed it down to three choices," he told her, setting three photos on the counter.

"This is a shaker style, obviously in white. This is a mission style in cherry, and this is an inset design in dark walnut," he told her, pointing to each picture in turn. "Of course, there are numerous other colors available in each of the styles—including birch and maple, which are both very popular."

Her gaze shifted from one picture to the next and back again. "I like the crisp, clean look of this one," she said, indicating the shaker style.

"It's a classic," he assured her.

"But I'm not sure about the white—more specifically, how it will hold up against sticky fingers."

"Peanut butter and jelly won't magically disappear, but they will wipe off easily."

"On the other hand, this dark walnut has real impact."

He smiled. "You're all over the map, aren't you?"

"I've been waiting a long time for this and I can't imagine that I'll ever want to redo the kitchen again, so I want to be sure that, whatever I choose, I'll be just as happy with it five or ten years from now as I am today."

"That makes sense," he agreed. "So why don't you hold on to the photos for now, but try to make a decision by Wednesday."

She nodded as she gathered up the photos and tucked them beneath the counter. "I'll let you know when I've decided, but it won't be before tomorrow. I'm working here until the store closes at eight tonight."

He scowled at that. "And then you've got to go home and pack up your kitchen?"

"Don't worry. Everything will be cleared out by the time your crew arrives in the morning," she assured him.

"I'm not as concerned about the cupboards as I am about you—that's a long day."

"I'm used to long days," she said.

The next words were out of his mouth before he considered what he was offering—or wondered why. "I could bring over some boxes later and help with the packing up."

"Thanks, but I can manage."

"I'm sure you can," he agreed. "But I don't understand why would you refuse the offer of free labor?"

"Because I learned the hard way that nothing in life is ever really free."

"Cynical, aren't you?"

"Realistic," she countered.

"You can call it what you want," he told her, "but you'll see me around nine."

She sighed. "Why are you doing this?"

He wasn't entirely sure of the answer to that question himself. Since she'd first opened the door to him on a rainy morning, he'd had more questions than answers. But for now, he only shrugged. "Maybe I feel guilty that I pushed you into agreeing to do the show without fully appreciating the impact it would have on your life."

"I am getting a new kitchen out of it," she reminded him.

He nodded. "And tonight, I'll help you clear out the old one."

Lauryn had found a few empty boxes in the storage room at The Locker Room, so she threw those into the back of the van when she finally left the store after closing up. Then she detoured to her parents' house again to pick up Kylie and Zachary, who had been fed and bathed and were all ready for bed. Still, she had barely finished tucking them in when she heard a soft knock at the back door.

Ryder had brought more boxes with him, and while she was still skeptical of the reasons behind his offer, she couldn't deny that he did provide the labor he'd promised. He started on the top cabinets while she concentrated her efforts on the bottom. And he meticulously itemized the contents of each box on the outside, then carried them into the dining room where he stacked them against an empty wall.

"What's all of this stuff?"

Lauryn looked up. "What stuff?"

He handed her an old shoe box. She lifted the lid to peek inside. "Oh. I'd almost forgotten about these."

"What are they?"

"Cookie cutters."

"That's a lot of cookie cutters."

She sifted through the metal shapes, her lips curving a little. "I used to bake a lot of cookies."

"Why?"

She shrugged and put the lid back on the box. "It was fun. My sisters and I used to bake and decorate cookies with our mom, and it was a tradition I'd always imagined sharing with my own kids. Of course, that was before I realized that simply taking care of the kids would take so much time."

"You don't bake anymore?"

"Rarely." She dropped the shoe box inside the larger box he was filling. "And when I do, they're not the kind that I decorate with icing and colored sugars. I should probably get rid of that stuff, but I keep thinking—or at least hoping—that I'll get back to it someday."

"Then you will," he said, opening another shoe box filled with icing bags, tips and various other utensils that he assumed were also for her cookie decorating. He packed it up and Lauryn returned to boxing up the everyday dishes.

"Did your mom bake cookies for you?" she asked.

"No."

The blunt, dismissive tone surprised her even more than the response. "Never?"

"She was always far too busy to concern herself with any kind of domestic or maternal duties."

"Busy doing what?" she wondered.

"Back then, I'm not sure—probably medical research of some kind. Now Dr. Cristina Tobin is a research supervisor at the Centers for Disease Control in Atlanta."

"Then maybe it's a good thing that she wasn't baking cookies for you when she came home from the lab," Lauryn said, making him smile.

"I'm sure that was her primary concern," he noted dryly.

"So your sister followed your mother's footsteps into medicine," she said, intrigued by this unexpected insight into his family. "Did your father work in construction?"

"No, he's a doctor, too. A cardiac surgeon at Emory."

"Wow," she said, clearly impressed. "But you had no interest in medicine?"

"Less than zero," he told her.

"A rebellion against your parents?"

He considered her question for a minute. "I don't think so. As soon as I got my first LEGO set, I always liked to build things, then knock them down and build them up again even better. Becoming a contractor seemed a natural progression from that."

"I'd say there are a lot of home owners who are extremely happy that you chose home renovations over medicine."

"Would you be one of them?"

"Maybe you should ask me that question after my new kitchen has been unveiled," she suggested.

"I will," he told her.

Although the baby monitor was up in Zachary's room, Kylie's scream came through loud and clear, followed by gulping sobs that twisted Lauryn's heart.

"Mama! Mama! Where are you, Mama?"

Lauryn raced up the stairs, anxious not only to alleviate

Kylie's growing panic but to quiet her before she managed to wake up her brother, too.

When she entered the room, she found her daughter sitting up in bed, her eyes wide and her cheeks streaked with tears.

"I'm here," Lauryn told her, lowering herself onto the edge of the mattress.

Kylie threw herself at Lauryn, sobbing against her chest. "I had a bad dweam, Mama."

She stroked a hand over her daughter's silky hair, gently untangling the twisted strands. "I know, honey. But the dream's over now and Mama's here."

"You stay wif me?"

"For a minute," she agreed.

Kylie scooted over to make room and patted the empty space on her pillow.

Lauryn hesitated, not wanting to be away from her kitchen assignment for too long but knowing her daughter would settle more easily if she stayed with her awhile. So she lay down beside her. "Close your eyes and go back to sleep, honey."

"You close your eyes," Kylie said.

So Lauryn did…for just a minute. Because comforting her children always comforted her, too. And maybe taking an extra minute away from the not just sexy but sweet Ryder Wallace would help her restore her equilibrium. Maybe.

Chapter Nine

Through the baby monitor on the counter, Ryder could hear the soft murmur of voices, though he couldn't hear the actual words. Kylie's outburst had given him quite a jolt, and before he even realized what was happening, Lauryn was racing up the stairs to her daughter.

He was surprised by the urge to follow her, to see for himself that everything was okay with the little girl. But it really wasn't any of his concern. Whatever monsters existed in Kylie's nightmares, he had no doubt that Lauryn would handle them. After only a short acquaintance with her, Ryder didn't doubt that she could handle anything.

Though she might look all soft and fragile, he knew that there was a steely strength beneath her silky skin. She was as much a warrior as a nurturer, and he was in danger of becoming infatuated with both parts of her.

He focused his attention on his task, pausing only to reply to a couple of text messages that came through on his cell phone. One from Arielle—a veterinarian assistant he'd dated for a few weeks in the summer—and two from Samantha—a high school gym teacher he'd gone out with exactly once. He replied to both that he was busy with work and unavailable for the foreseeable future, without a hint of regret that it was true.

Even before *Ryder to the Rescue* had made him a pseudo-celebrity, he'd attracted a fair amount of attention from women, and he couldn't deny that he'd enjoyed his popularity. His sister had occasionally accused him of enjoying it too much. But he was always honest about what he wanted and he always treated the women he dated with respect. Recently, though, he'd found himself starting to grow weary of the whole dating scene and wondering if he wasn't ready for something more.

He immediately shook his head, appalled that such a thought would even cross his mind. Of course, he wasn't weary of the dating scene. Short-term relationships were the hallmark of his life; commitments and entanglements were to be avoided at all costs. Then his thoughts drifted to the mother who was upstairs now, soothing her frightened child, and he acknowledged that there might be circumstances in which the benefits exceeded the costs.

Ryder pushed the tempting thought aside. He was nearly finished in the kitchen when Lauryn made her way back downstairs.

"I'm so sorry," she said. "I just snuggled with Kylie for a few minutes, to make sure she was settled, and I guess I fell asleep, too."

"That's okay," he told her. "I managed to carry on without you."

She looked at the stacked and labeled boxes, then at the empty cupboards. "I feel like the shoemaker who wakes up to discover the elves have done all of his work."

"You still have to figure out where you want everything in the dining room," he told her. "But that can wait until the morning."

"Thank you."

"Is Kylie okay?" he asked, sincerely concerned about the terror he'd heard in the little girl's voice.

Lauryn nodded. "She's sleeping soundly now."

"Does she often have bad dreams?"

"Not so much recently—thank God," she told him. "But for a while, she was waking up almost every night, and occasionally several times in one night."

"Any idea what triggers that?"

"You mean other than her father suddenly disappearing from her life?"

He winced. "I guess that would do it."

She nodded. "The pediatrician has assured me that it's a fairly normal response to what she's been through and that she'll eventually outgrow them."

"Was she okay last Saturday night—at her sleepover?"

"She was," Lauryn confirmed. "Which is a big step. She used to love staying at my parents' house, but sleepovers have been few and far between over the past nine months."

He could understand that Kylie would want to stick close to the one parent she had left, and he wondered again about the kind of man who could walk away from not only his wife but his beautiful daughter and unborn son. His own parents had hardly been role models, but they'd accepted the responsibilities of parenthood—or at least those they couldn't abdicate to the nanny.

"It's hard to see the changes in her," Lauryn admitted softly. "She was always an outgoing and affectionate child who never shied away from strangers."

"She certainly didn't shy away from me," he noted. "Even on day one, after you'd closed the door in my face, she invited me to have tea with her."

Lauryn smiled a little at the memory. "Well, you did give her flowers. A girl never forgets the first boy who gives her flowers."

He didn't know if that was true, but he liked to think the little girl would remember him when he was gone. And as soon as the kitchen was done, he would be gone, so it would be crazy to even think about starting something with Lauryn. But he couldn't deny that he was tempted.

"Everything changed after Rob left," she said, picking up the thread of their previous conversation. "She started to panic anytime I was out of her sight. I was in the hospital for two nights when Zachary was born, and she was almost inconsolable during that time."

"Who stayed with her then?"

"She stayed with my parents." Lauryn went to the fridge—relocated to the dining room—and retrieved a bottle of chardonnay, then looked around as if trying to remember what she'd done with the wineglasses. Since he'd packed them away, he found the box easily.

"You're not having one?" she asked, when he handed her a glass.

"Are you offering to share?"

"Sure."

So he retrieved a second glass and poured wine for himself while Lauryn sipped hers.

"My parents have been so great through this whole thing," she told him. "Actually, my whole family's been great, but my parents have gone above and beyond."

Although he had no personal experience with that kind of support, he knew that family were supposed to be the people to turn to in a time of crisis. He couldn't imagine ever relying on either of his parents, but he knew his sister would be there for him—as he would for her.

"My mom understood Kylie's apprehension, but she also believed that her granddaughter needed to stop clinging to me twenty-four/seven. When Zachary was about six months old, she planned a special day for Kylie. She and my dad took her to the zoo in Asheville, then to Buster Bear's and finally back to their house for the night."

"Any three-year-old's fantasy," he remarked with a smile.

She sipped her wine, then nodded. "And Kylie had a fabulous time—until she found out that she was sleeping over. Then she had a complete meltdown. She cried and screamed, but my mother remained firm. She told Kylie that she could call me to say good-night, but only if she stopped crying."

"Sounds like tough love."

"A little tougher than I was prepared for," Lauryn admitted. "I understood what she was doing, that she wanted Kylie to learn to trust that I would be there in the morning, but it was so hard for me to hear my little girl fighting against tears." She smiled wryly. "I don't think any of us slept that night, but the panic attacks finally started to fade. In fact, this is the first one she's had in several weeks."

"But when they happen, they upset you as much as they upset her," he guessed.

"When you're a parent, there's nothing worse than a child who is hurting—especially when you can't do anything about it."

Maybe a parent like Lauryn, but he already knew that she was one of a kind. He touched her hand, and her quick intake of breath confirmed that she wasn't oblivious to the chemistry between them, either.

"But you are doing something," he told her, as she carefully drew her hand away from his. "You're showing her that she can depend on you to be there for her."

She lifted her glass to her lips again, swallowed the final sip. "I'm not sure that's much consolation to a little girl who's missing her daddy."

He tipped the bottle, emptying the last of the wine into her glass. "Do you miss him, too?"

Ryder wasn't sure what compelled him to ask the question, except that he wanted to know. When she'd first told him that her husband was gone, she'd said that she wasn't sorry. But she'd been on the defensive that day, and he wondered if she'd held back her true feelings.

"I got used to Rob not being here a long time before he ever left," she told him. "When he packed up and moved out, it was almost a relief, because I could finally stop pretending that everything was normal. And then, of course, I felt guilty for being relieved, because of Kylie and Zachary."

"Divorce is hardly uncommon today," he pointed out to her.

"It is in my family," she retorted. "My parents have been married thirty-nine years, and both of my father's brothers have been married to their wives for more than forty. And all of my cousins who are married—and most of them are—have figured out how to make it work.

"Well, Matt was divorced from his first wife," she acknowledged. "But that wasn't his fault."

"There doesn't have to be fault," Ryder told her. "Sometimes things just don't work out."

"Are you speaking from personal experience?" she challenged.

He nodded. "I was around Kylie's age when my parents split up."

The confession succeeded in banking some of the fire in her eyes, and when she spoke again, her tone was more curious than confrontational. "Do you remember much from that time?"

"It's hard to separate what I actually remember from what I've been told, but it wasn't particularly traumatic. We were living in Brookhaven at the time, so my mom chose to move out, to get a place closer to the Northeast Georgia Medical Center, where she was working."

Her forehead crinkled. "Your mother left—and left you and your sister behind?"

He smiled at the outrage in her voice. "We were well taken care of," he assured her.

"By your father?"

"By the nanny," he clarified. "And when my mom was settled again, she and my dad shared custody, which meant that we moved back and forth every two weeks."

"How was that?" she asked curiously.

He shrugged. "It was the status quo, as far as I knew, and Hennie moved back and forth with us."

"That's one good thing about Rob moving to California," she said. "At least there wasn't any fighting over custody."

"I have a feeling he wouldn't have stood a chance."

She managed a smile at that, and the sweet curve of her lips seemed to arrow straight to his heart—which was Ryder's cue to make his escape, before he became even more mired in his unbidden awareness of Lauryn.

He finished his wine and set the empty glass on the table. She automatically rose to her feet as he did. "Thank you—for all of your help tonight."

"You're welcome."

"I guess I'll see you in the morning," she said, following him to the door.

"You will," he confirmed, but he hesitated with his hand on the knob.

When he looked at her again, he saw in her expression a combination of awareness and wariness. The former tempted him to move closer; the latter propelled him to walk away.

He did so, already counting the hours.

Friday afternoon, Lauryn enlisted Jordyn to babysit Kylie and Zachary while she went into Raleigh to meet with Adam Carr, a former assistant manager of The Locker Room. The college student had worked for Rob for four years before taking a job at a bigger store in the bigger city. At least, that was her ex-husband's explanation for his employee's departure. When she'd crossed paths with Adam a few weeks earlier, she'd discovered that the truth was a little bit different.

Adam had left The Locker Room because he had a lot of ideas to generate more business for the store and he was frustrated by Rob's refusal to hear them. Lauryn was desperate for ideas and eager to listen, and after their conversation, she'd immediately offered him a management position.

All the way home, she anticipated sharing the details with her sister. But when she pulled into her driveway, Jordyn's car wasn't there.

Lauryn hurried into the house, halting abruptly in the entrance of the living room where Kylie was kneeling on the floor, a coloring book and crayons on the coffee table in front of her, and Zachary was asleep in his playpen, his favorite blanket clutched in one hand, the thumb of the other in his mouth.

She pressed a hand to her racing heart and released an unsteady breath. Her children were here. They were fine.

And sitting on the sofa, watching over them, was Ryder.

"Where's Jordyn?" she asked, when she managed to catch her breath again.

"She got a call from the author she works with—something about an emergency last-minute revision—and said she had to go."

Lauryn was incredulous. "And she just left?"

"Only after she asked me to hang around until you got home," he explained.

"I'm so sorry," Lauryn said. "She never should have imposed on you that way."

"It's okay," he assured her. "Your sister had somewhere to be. I didn't."

But Lauryn had deliberately stayed away until she was sure he'd be gone, because after the time they'd spent together Monday night, she'd worried that she'd shared too much. Revealed too much. And the insights he'd given her into his own family had changed her perspective on him. He wasn't just America's Hottest Handyman to her now— he was a real person, with real-life experiences and scars. And it was that man she was drawn to more and more every time she was near him.

"Well, thank you for staying, but I'm sure you want to get home now, and I need to get supper on."

"Wyder said we can have pizza," Kylie chimed in.

Lauryn shook her head. "Not tonight, honey. I've got spaghetti sauce in the freezer—"

"Pizza," her daughter insisted.

She sighed. "Kylie, please don't do this now."

"But Wyder—"

"Should have checked with your mom first," he said to the little girl. Then he addressed Lauryn, his tone apologetic. "But it's already ordered."

She sighed, a little frustrated at the unexpected changes to their usual routine. "You definitely should have checked with me first."

"I know, but we were hungry and I didn't know when you would be home."

Which she knew wasn't unreasonable from his perspective, but the whole situation had caught her off guard. She'd come home expecting to find her sister with her kids—not the man who'd rescued Kylie's mural from ruin and fixed her roof and stirred feelings inside of her that she didn't want to have stirred.

But maybe it wasn't surprising that she was attracted to him. In the space of a week, he'd done more to help around the house than her ex-husband had done in a year—maybe even six years. And now he was hanging out with her children, and looking not just at ease but as if he belonged.

"In fact," Ryder said, in response to the peal of the doorbell, "that's probably our dinner now."

Holding back another sigh, she reached for her purse, wondering if the delivery person would take her credit card to pay for the pizza—and silently crossing her fingers that it wasn't maxed out because she'd relied on it to cover other essentials, such as groceries and gas for her car.

"I've got it," he said, moving past her with cash in hand.

She should insist on paying for the meal. But the truth was, she didn't even have twenty dollars in her wallet and she'd rather not run up her credit card. Which meant that she had to accept his offer—and that he would be staying to eat with them.

"It looks like you ordered more than just pizza," she said when he returned with the food.

"I got some wings and Caesar salad, too," he told her. "Because Kylie said it was her favorite and I figured you'd want her to have some kind of vegetable."

Which was true, but not something she would have expected him to consider. "I also want her to go wash up," she said, looking pointedly at her daughter.

Kylie, eager for pizza, obediently scampered off.

"Do you want this in the dining room?" Ryder asked.

"Yes, please." She headed to the bookcase that was serving as a makeshift cabinet while her kitchen was under construction. "I'll get plates."

"There should be paper plates and plastic cutlery in the bag," he told her.

"You really did think of everything," she noted.

"I know it can't be easy carting your dishes downstairs to the laundry tub."

"It's not easy, but it works. And it's only for a few more weeks, right?" she asked, her tone hopeful.

She was managing well enough with her refrigerator, microwave and toaster oven set up in the dining room, but after only four days, she was already missing a real kitchen—and excited about the unveiling of the completed job.

Ryder's crew had completed the demolition work in the first two days, filling a Dumpster in the backyard with her old cabinets and the ugly brown linoleum—even pieces of drywall and chunks of wood that suggested bigger changes than she'd anticipated. But since she'd approved the basic layout, picked out her cabinets, countertops, backsplash, floor tile and lighting fixtures, she'd been banned from the area.

In fact, the director was so determined to ensure that she not get a glimpse of the work until they'd finished, he'd closed off the doorways from the kitchen to the hallway and dining room and covered the inside of the kitchen windows with dark paper.

"All clean," Kylie announced, holding up her dripping hands for her mother to see.

"Yes, but you missed the drying that usually comes after washing."

Her daughter wiped her hands down the front of her pink overalls, then held them up again.

Lauryn shook her head as Ryder bit back a smile. "Take a seat."

While Kylie climbed into her booster seat, Lauryn got the milk out of the fridge and poured a cup for her.

Kylie ate one slice of pizza—but not the crust. She also had a helping of Caesar salad. Of course, Zachary woke up as soon as Lauryn took the first bite out of her own pizza, so she got up to change his diaper, then settled him in his high chair at the table. While she warmed up some leftover roast beef, mashed potatoes and corn, she let him chew on Kylie's abandoned crust, keeping a close eye on him to ensure he didn't manage to tear off any pieces.

When she returned to the table, Ryder was putting more salad on Kylie's plate.

"An' that one," Kylie said, pointing to a crouton.

Ryder scooped it out with the tongs and set it on top of the salad already on her plate.

"An' that one." She pointed to another, which he dutifully scooped out for her.

"An' that one."

"And that's all," Lauryn said firmly when Ryder had added the last crouton to her plate.

Kylie picked up her fork.

"How's your pizza?" Ryder asked Lauryn.

"It's really good."

He gestured to her plate. "So why aren't you eating it?"

"Sorry, I guess my mind was wandering." But she picked up her slice and took another bite.

"Anything you want to talk about?"

She shook her head as she continued to chew.

"I'm all done, Mama," Kylie said.

Lauryn glanced at her daughter's plate. "You didn't eat any of the salad you said you wanted."

"I ate the cwoutons."

"Did you drink your milk?"

Kylie nodded.

"Okay, you can go wash up again—and dry this time," she reminded her daughter, who was already climbing down from the table.

"'Kay."

"You really should let me pay you for dinner," she said to Ryder.

"I would have ordered all of this even if I wasn't sharing it," he told her.

"Even the salad?"

"Maybe not the salad," he acknowledged. "But if it makes you feel better, you can consider this payback for the meat loaf you shared with me last week."

It might have made her feel better, except that he'd only been at her house on meat loaf night because he'd spent the afternoon putting up tarps on her roof. But before she could say anything else, Kylie wheeled a pink case into the room.

"You play Barbie wif me, Wyder?"

"Sure," Ryder agreed easily.

Kylie beamed at him and opened the case, spilling dolls and clothes and accessories onto the floor. "I fowgot

Darcy," she said, and raced up to her bedroom to retrieve her favorite doll.

"She named all of her Barbies after the girls in her preschool class," Lauryn explained. "Darcy is currently her best friend."

"Well, it never made any sense to me that they'd all be named Barbie," Ryder said.

"You've given this matter some thought, have you?" she asked, amused by his matter-of-fact statement.

"I had an older sister growing up," he reminded her. "I spent a lot of time playing with Barbies."

She couldn't picture the strong, broad-shouldered man sitting across from her playing with skinny plastic dolls. "You did?"

He nodded. "I had to if I wanted Avery to catch for me while I practiced pitching for Little League."

Kylie came skipping back into the room with Darcy.

"You play, too, Mama?"

"No, thanks. I'll let you and Ryder play while I give Zachary his bath."

After her little guy was bathed, diapered and dressed in a one-piece sleeper, she went downstairs to fix his bottle. By the time she had it ready, he was rubbing his fists against his eyes.

"Clean up your toys, Kylie—it's your turn in the tub next."

"Perfect timing," Ryder said. "Darcy and Ken were just getting ready to go to bed."

Lauryn's brows lifted.

"I mean—each to their own beds," he hastened to clarify. "In their separate houses."

"But they're gettin' mawied tomowow," Kylie said. "Then they can live in the same house."

"Tomorrow? That doesn't give you a lot of time to plan the big event," Lauryn told her. "And you definitely need to pack up all of her clothes and shoes before you can have a wedding."

The little girl immediately began shoving everything back into her pink case. "I can't find the weddin' dwess, Mama."

"I'm sure it's around here somewhere."

"She can't get mawied wifout a weddin' dwess."

"We'll find it tomorrow," Lauryn promised.

Zachary squirmed, reaching for his bottle, and Ryder held out his arms, offering. Lauryn hesitated.

"You can hardly feed him and bathe Kylie at the same time," he pointed out.

"Not very easily," she agreed. And not without Kylie splashing around so much that Zachary would likely need to be changed again, so she passed the bottle and the baby to him.

Zachary had other men in his life: his grandfather and Jordyn's husband—Uncle Marco—and numerous other honorary uncles who were actually her cousins, so maybe it wasn't surprising that he'd immediately taken to Ryder. But still it unsettled Lauryn to see her baby nestled so contentedly in his strong arms.

"Do you mind if I turn on the television so we can watch the baseball game?"

"Go ahead," she said. "Baseball usually helps him fall asleep."

Ryder gasped. "Say it ain't so."

"If I did, I'd be lying."

He looked down at the baby, who was looking at him with wide blue eyes. "Well, you're young yet," he decided. "Your opinion will change when you're strong enough to hold a bat."

"I don't think that's going to happen anytime soon," she told him. "He's only just started holding his bottle."

Chapter Ten

Lauryn wasn't surprised to find that Zachary was asleep by the time she'd tucked Kylie into bed, read her a quick story and returned downstairs. She *was* surprised to find that Ryder had fallen asleep, too, with the baby securely tucked against his chest.

Rob had never sat and cuddled with his daughter like that. He'd held her, usually when Lauryn had thrust the baby into his arms and didn't give him a choice, but he'd always claimed he felt awkward and afraid of hurting her. She didn't know anyone who was stronger than Ryder or who had such an appealing softer side. The combination was incredibly enticing. The fact that he'd actually sat on the floor playing Barbies with her little girl made him almost irresistible.

The attraction she could deal with. As she'd told her sister, there likely wasn't a woman between seventeen and seventy who didn't find him attractive. But the more time she spent with him, the more she found herself drawn to his kindness and generosity and thinking of him not as a TV star but simply a man. A man who made her remember that she wasn't just a mother but a woman, too.

But Lauryn was determined to resist his magnetism. Her life was already complicated enough without adding a new man to the mix. Not that she had any reason to believe that was even an option. Aside from some lighthearted banter and the occasional flirtatious smile, he'd given her no indication that the attraction she felt might be shared.

Ryder's eyes opened when she lifted the baby's weight off his chest.

"Obviously, the game wasn't stimulating enough to keep even you awake," she said lightly.

"The Braves are winning," he told her.

"What's the score?"

"Five-three, top of the sixth."

"Six-three, bottom of the seventh," she informed him. "One on and one out."

"You know baseball?" Ryder sounded surprised.

"I dated a varsity third baseman in high school."

"Did he get to third base with you?" he asked, with a teasing smile.

She just shook her head, not willing to discuss her romantic past with a man who made her wish she had a romantic present. "I'm going to take Zachary up to his crib now."

The baby was in such a deep sleep he didn't stir when she settled him in his bed and covered him with a light blanket. She lightly stroked a finger over his cheek and sent up a silent prayer of thanks for her good fortune. In his short life, he'd given her very little cause for concern—and endless joy.

She checked on Kylie again before she headed downstairs, happy to see that she was sound asleep, too, her favorite stuffed dog tucked under her arm.

"Thank you for babysitting," she said to Ryder when she returned to the living room. "And for the pizza."

"It was my pleasure."

She smiled at the automatic response. "I'm sure you had more exciting plans for your Friday night, but I appreciate that you stayed."

"Actually, I didn't have any plans at all," he told her, sounding a little surprised by the fact himself. "And I quite enjoyed hanging out with you and the kids."

"I have to confess, as much as I love Kylie and Zachary, it's nice to have some adult company every once in a while."

"And it was nice for me to be able to pretend to be a kid again for a little while," he said.

"I know that you're Kylie's new BFF," she confided. "Even I don't have the patience to play Barbies with her for as long as you did."

He grinned. "We're more than BFFs—she asked me to marry her."

"Well, you gave her flowers, stopped it from raining in her castle and played with her," Lauryn reminded him. "Of course, she's head over heels in love with you."

"Is that all it takes?" he wondered aloud.

"For a three-year-old," she confirmed.

He leaned forward and settled his hands on her knees. Even through the denim, she felt the heat of his touch—a heat that quickly spread through her whole body. "What about the three-year-old's mom?"

"Are you flirting with me?" she asked, not sure if she was more wary or hopeful.

One side of his mouth tipped up in a wry smile. "If you have to ask, obviously my skills are rusty."

"It's more likely that mine are," she admitted, feeling more than a little out of her element.

"Then maybe we should work on changing that," he suggested, as his hands skimmed her outer thighs.

It was a friendly caress, not overtly sexual in any way. But to a woman who hadn't been touched by a man in a very long time, the casual slide of his palms over the soft denim was both erotic and enticing.

"Why?" she asked, the question barely more than a whisper.

His gaze held hers as his lips curved again. "Because flirting is only one of the many fun things that men and women can do together."

"But why are you flirting with *me*?" she asked.

"Because you're a beautiful and intriguing woman."

And he was seducing her with nothing more than his eyes and his voice, and she wasn't ready to be seduced.

"I'm a mess," Lauryn told him, trying to ground herself back in reality again. "My life is a mess. Surely, in the past week, you've figured that out."

"Yeah, but you're a hot mess."

She managed a smile. "Flatterer."

He must have sensed the shift in her mood, because he lifted his hands away and reached for something on the sofa. "By the way—" he held up one of Kylie's Barbies "—I found this stuck between the cushions."

"That's the wedding dress she was looking for."

"But she's still missing the veil."

"You're quite the expert on Barbie's wardrobe," she teased, grateful for the change of topic and the lessening of the tension between them. "I'm starting to believe that you really did play with your sister's dolls when you were a kid."

"I wouldn't make something like that up," he assured her.

"Well, I think it's pretty cool that your parents let you play with Barbies and let Avery play baseball without trying to force gender stereotypes on you," she noted.

"A consequence of absenteeism rather than open-mindedness," he assured her. "My guess is that they both thought parenthood would be an interesting experiment— and then they lost interest in it."

This time she reached out to him, touching a tentative hand to his arm. "I'm sorry."

He shrugged. "It wasn't so bad," he said. "Because when you're a kid, you think all families are like your own."

"Not everyone is cut out to be a parent," she acknowledged, her ex-husband having proven that to her.

Then, because she regretted introducing the unhappy

topic, she shifted their conversation in another direction. "I've been watching your show."

His brows lifted. "Why?"

"I was curious."

"You were checking my references," he accused, but his tone was light, teasing.

"That might have been part of it, too," she acknowledged.

"And what did you think?"

"I think they really like the close-ups of you in tight T-shirts."

His gaze shifted away, as if he was embarrassed by her observation. "According to Virginia Gennings—the producer—we have a strong female demographic."

"I'm not surprised," she told him.

"And women are more likely to push their husbands to make changes around the house, while most men are content with the status quo and resistant to change."

"How did Virginia Gennings discover that you look good in a tool belt?"

"I built a solarium for a client in Winston-Salem. We were just finishing up the project when her sister came to town for a visit. Virginia was that sister."

"It was that easy?"

He grinned. "I guess that would depend on who you ask. Virginia would say it wasn't easy at all. She'd apparently pitched the idea to the studio and got the green light, but when she pitched it to me, I turned her down."

"Why?" she asked, genuinely interested in his reasons.

"First, I'm not a fan of reality TV shows in general. Second, I'm a contractor, not an actor. Third, I started my own business because I like being my own boss, so I wasn't keen to work for someone else again."

"What changed your mind?" Lauryn asked.

"She wouldn't take no for an answer," he admitted. "She

thought I was holding out for more money. She came back three times with more lucrative contracts before she realized that what I really wanted was some degree of control over my life.

"So I got the big paycheck, a one-year contract, the right to choose the projects and my crew, final approval of editing and the option to bail if I didn't like what they were doing with the show."

"And now the show's in its sixth season?"

He nodded. "Because we film two seasons a year. Your reno will air at the end of season seven."

She was excited about the renovation, but not so much to know that her friends and neighbors and hundreds of thousands of strangers would be able to watch it on TV.

"So tell me what you've been doing while we've been tearing apart your kitchen," Ryder suggested.

"Mostly trying to find someone else to manage The Locker Room," she admitted. "Soon to be 'Sports Destination— where your quest for the right equipment ends.' And, in smaller letters, 'A Garrett Family Business.'"

He considered the slogan for a minute, then nodded. "It's catchy."

"But not too cheesy?" she asked hopefully.

"Not too cheesy," he assured her. "But maybe you should consider 'where your quest for the *perfect* equipment ends'—it sets a higher standard."

"Oh, I like that. And Tristyn will be so irked that she didn't think of it."

He raised a brow.

"The new name and slogan were her ideas," she said, answering the unspoken question. "Of course, PR is her specialty. She said it was going to be enough of a challenge to bring customers into the store without having to fight against their preconceptions about The Locker Room."

"She's right," he agreed.

"I balked initially," she admitted. "It almost seemed like cheating, using my family's name, as if I was trying to capitalize on the goodwill that they've built up in this town over the past fifty years."

"Isn't it your name, too?"

"The one I was born with, anyway. And the one I shared with my sisters for a lot of years, which I guess makes it appropriate for our joint venture."

"You're lucky to have the support of your family."

She knew it was true. And she knew that Ryder hadn't been nearly as fortunate.

From what he'd told her about his sister, she could tell they were close. From what he'd revealed about his parents, she guessed they were not. And while she was undeniably curious, she was also determined to respect the boundaries of their professional relationship.

Even if those boundaries had already shifted more than a little bit.

After meeting with Adam early Saturday morning to hand off the keys to her new store manager and review the tasks that needed immediate attention, Lauryn happily left him in charge and headed over to her sister's house.

Lauryn took two minutes to set up Zachary's playpen and put the television on for Kylie before she joined her sister in the kitchen of the new home she shared with her husband.

"Coffee?" Jordyn offered. "I picked up some of that cinnamon one you like."

"Okay," she agreed. "But that's not getting you off the hook for last night."

Her sister dropped the pod into the brewer. "What did I do last night?"

"You were supposed to be watching Kylie and Zachary. Instead, you left them in the care of a virtual stranger."

"Ryder's not a stranger," Jordyn denied.

"He was until ten days ago," she pointed out.

"And in that short span of time, your children have come to adore him."

"They adore everyone."

Her sister nodded, conceding the point. "And when I couldn't figure out why Zachary wouldn't stop fussing, Ryder suggested that I give him a teething biscuit—which worked like a charm."

"My mistake," she said dryly. "Obviously, the man is a childcare expert."

"And even if he's not," Jordyn said, "Kylie and Zachary appear relatively unscathed."

She wrapped her hands around the mug her sister passed to her. "That's hardly the point."

"What *is* your point?"

"If you really had to leave, you should have called *me*."

"I was going to," Jordyn said. "But I knew you were in Raleigh, and then Ryder offered to hang around. By the way, how did things go with Adam?"

"Now you're trying to sidetrack me," Lauryn accused.

"No, I'm trying to find out if you persuaded the former assistant manager to come back."

"He's the manager now," she said. "I handed over the keys this morning."

"Well, that's a huge step in the right direction," her sister said.

"It will free up a lot of my time," Lauryn agreed. "I felt so guilty for dumping the kids on Mom every time I turned around. Which, incidentally, is why I asked *you* to take care of them yesterday."

"So…how did Ryder screw up?" Jordyn asked cautiously.

"What do you mean?" She lifted the mug to her lips.

"I assume you came in here all fired up because he'd done something wrong."

"No, he didn't do anything wrong," she admitted.

"Then why are you scowling?"

"Because..." She faltered, aware that her explanation wasn't going to sound rational or reasonable—and probably wasn't rational or reasonable. "Because he was so good with both of them."

"And that's a problem...why?" Jordyn prompted.

She sighed. "I know it shouldn't be, and you're probably going to tell me I'm being ridiculous—"

"You're being ridiculous," her sister confirmed.

"—but he scares me."

Jordyn's teasing immediately gave way to concern. "What do you mean? What did he do?"

"I don't mean that I'm afraid of him," she hastened to clarify, wary of the warrior gleam in her sister's eyes. "But I am afraid of the way he makes feel."

Jordyn relaxed again. "How does he make you feel?"

Lauryn didn't know if there was a simple answer to that question. For the past year and a half, as her efforts to save her crumbling marriage had ended with the acceptance of its demise, she'd gone through the motions. She'd focused on her daughter and preparations for the new baby, her emotions with respect to her husband mostly numb.

Ryder had awakened those long-dormant emotions, and she wasn't entirely sure that was a good thing.

"Unsettled," she finally responded.

"Hmm," Jordyn mused.

"What does *that* mean?" she asked warily.

"I'm getting the impression that he didn't rush off when you got home last night."

She shook her head. "He'd already ordered pizza for dinner, then he stayed to eat with us. Then he played with

Kylie while I got Zachary ready for bed, and he gave Zachary his bottle while Kylie had her bath."

"Wow," Jordyn said. "In one night, he acted more like a husband and father than your ex-husband ever did."

She nodded. "And it scares me to realize that there's a part of me that still wants that. And how crazy is it that I can actually envision this man—who I barely know—in that role?"

"I don't think it's crazy at all," her sister told her. "You deserve to be happy, Laur. And if he makes you happy, then you should go for it."

She shook her head. "My divorce was finalized three weeks ago. There's no way I should be thinking about—"

"Your divorce *is* final," Jordyn interjected. "It's okay for you to move on."

"I have moved on."

"Prove it."

"I have a new business partnership with my sisters and I'm having my kitchen renovated—isn't that proof enough?"

"No," Jordyn said bluntly. "You should do something to thank Ryder for babysitting last night."

"I said thank you. Several times, in fact."

The music emanating from the television in the other room warned that Kylie's favorite program had ended. As if on cue, her daughter skipped into the kitchen—and directly to the cupboard beside the stove.

"What are you doing?" Lauryn asked her.

"Gwyff wantsa tweat," she said, referring to Jordyn's tailless, one-eyed cat. The creature was notoriously anti-social but highly food-motivated, which made him willing to tolerate anyone who fed him. He tolerated Kylie extremely well.

"Gryff always wants treats," Jordyn noted.

"Can I give him tweats?" Kylie asked.

"One treat," her aunt instructed.

"'Kay," the little girl agreed, reaching into the box.

"Speaking of treats," Jordyn said, "I think the situation calls for cupcakes."

"Cupcakes?" Kylie echoed hopefully.

"What situation?" Lauryn asked warily.

"The Ryder situation."

Lauryn shook her head. "He's not a situation and I'm not baking cupcakes."

"I like cupcakes," Kylie chimed in. "Choc'ate cupcakes."

"I know, honey. And Gryff would really like his treat now," Lauryn said, urging her daughter back to the living room.

But, of course, the cat—even with half an ear missing—had heard the box of treats being opened and had come to find Kylie, who simply opened up her hand and let Gryff have his snack.

"See? Even Kylie's in favor of the plan," Jordyn said.

Still, Lauryn hesitated. "I don't want to send the wrong message."

"That you're grateful to him for looking after your kids?"

"And I don't have a kitchen," she pointed out.

"You could use this one."

"I suppose you have all the ingredients I'd need, too?" she challenged.

"Probably not," Jordyn admitted. "But I can pop out to the grocery store."

"I thought you were in a hurry to run errands."

"And the grocery store errand just moved to the top of the list. What do you need to make cupcakes?"

"Spwinkles," Kylie chimed in. "We needs lots an' lotsa spwinkles."

Even as Lauryn added the necessary ingredients to her sister's list, she wondered if the cupcakes were somehow going to say a lot more than a simple "thank you." And was that a message she was ready to send?

Chapter Eleven

Ryder's morning didn't start out too badly. After a meeting with the production team, he went for breakfast with Owen and Virginia. The waitress at the Morning Glory Café brought his breakfast platter with a candle in it, undoubtedly Virginia's idea. The show's producer never missed a detail.

As he was driving away from the restaurant, his phone rang. When he connected the call, he was greeted by his sister singing "Happy Birthday," loudly and off-key.

"I'm on my way to the airport," he said when Avery paused to take a breath. "Isn't that punishment enough without adding your singing to the mix?"

"Actually, that's the other reason I called," his sister said. "To tell you that your chauffeur services aren't required."

It was possible that Justin had changed his shift at the hospital and was available to meet his mother-in-law's flight, but Ryder suspected otherwise. "She's not coming, is she?"

"No," Avery admitted.

He shook his head. Just when he thought his mother couldn't disappoint him anymore, she proved otherwise. Her last-minute cancellation didn't bother him—meetings with his mother were inevitably awkward and strained—but he knew that Avery had been looking forward to her visit. More importantly, she'd been looking forward to Vanessa meeting her maternal grandmother.

"Did she say why?"

"The usual."

Which, of course, meant work. Nothing mattered more to Dr. Cristina Tobin—not even her children. Ryder used to admire her dedication—he'd certainly been told often enough that her research was important, that what she did saved lives. Now it just made him sad. Maybe she did save lives, but she did so at the cost of living her own.

"Are you okay?" he asked his sister now.

"Of course, I'm okay," she said, her tone just a little too bright. "It's not as if I didn't know this might happen."

"Just because you're not surprised doesn't mean you're not disappointed."

"You're right," she admitted. "And I was a little disappointed at first. Then I called Justin's mom and dad and invited them to come for dinner tonight because I'd already bought the groceries to make chicken piccata, and Ellen was absolutely thrilled by the invitation because they haven't seen their granddaughter in three whole days."

"Three whole days, huh?"

Avery chuckled. "Are you feeling guilty now that it's been seven days since you stopped by?"

"I'll see you soon," he promised.

"You could come tonight, too," she offered. "There's going to be plenty of food."

"I told you—I have plans for tonight."

"I remember that's what you said," she acknowledged. "I just wasn't sure you were sticking with that story now that our mother isn't going to be in town."

"I'm sticking with that story," he told her.

"Well, I hope you have a wonderful birthday, little brother."

"Thanks, big sis." He disconnected the call and turned his vehicle around.

He hadn't been completely honest when he told his sister he had plans, but he was optimistic. He knew any number of women who would happily make themselves available to celebrate his birthday, but he didn't want to celebrate with any of them. Instead he drove to the lumber yard, because he wasn't opposed to a little bit of manipulation to get what he wanted.

He was hammering the final replacement board into place in the front porch when Lauryn's van pulled into the driveway. He quickly moved his tools and debris away from the door so that she could get to it without tripping over anything.

Kylie walked beside her mother, balancing a covered plastic container in her hands. Lauryn was weighted down with a diaper bag and purse over her shoulder, the baby's car seat in one hand and three grocery bags in the other. He dumped his tool belt and went to meet her.

"Do you not understand the concept of a day off?" she asked in lieu of a greeting.

"I like to fix things," he told her.

"Then you've definitely come to the right place."

He grinned at that. "Can I give you a hand with something, since both of yours appear to be full?"

She jiggled the keys that were dangling from a finger. "If you could open the door, that would be great."

He did as she requested, then took Zachary's car seat from her, too.

"Thanks," she said. "I swear he's getting heavier every day."

"He's got a few pounds on my niece, that's for sure."

"He's also six months older than Vanessa," Lauryn pointed out. To Kylie, she said, "Go put those on the table in the dining room, please."

The little girl did as she was requested, then turned to Ryder. "We made cupcakes for you."

"For me?" he asked, surprised.

She nodded.

"As a thank-you for last night," Lauryn said, starting to put her groceries away.

"You already said thank you," he reminded her, unbuckling Zachary's restraints and lifting him out of his car seat. "And how did you make cupcakes without an oven?"

"Jordyn let us use hers."

She was still busy with her groceries, so he gently laid the sleeping baby down in his playpen. "What kind of cupcakes?"

"Choc'ate," Kylie chimed in.

"We made vanilla, too," Lauryn said. "Because we didn't know what you'd like."

"Chocolate are my favorite."

"Me, too," the little girl told him.

He smiled. "Did you help make them?"

She nodded. "I put on the icin' an' spwinkles."

"Sprinkles, too? You must have known it was my birthday."

Lauryn closed the fridge and turned to him. "It's your birthday—today?"

He nodded.

"Why didn't you tell me?"

He shrugged. "It didn't exactly come up in conversation."

"We needs birfday candles," Kylie told her mother.

"You're right," Lauryn agreed. "Let's see if I can remember where I put them."

She put on a pot of coffee first, and it only took her a minute after that to find the candles and matches—tucked away on the top shelf of the bookcase, far out of reach of her children. Then she selected one of the chocolate cupcakes—with lots of sprinkles on top—and set it on a plate before inserting a single blue-and-white-striped candle into the middle of it.

Kylie looked at the candle, then at Ryder. "I fink he needs more candles," her daughter whispered to Lauryn.

"I think you're right," she whispered back. "But the number of candles he needs probably wouldn't fit on a cupcake."

"How many candles are you, Wyder?"

He smiled at her phrasing of the question. "Twenty-eight," he told her.

"Thatsa lotta candles," Kylie said solemnly.

"Of course, it seems like a lot to her," Lauryn explained. "She just learned to count to ten—and sometimes she skips over nine."

But he could tell the number had surprised her, too, prompting him to ask, "Do you think it's a lot of candles?"

"It's fewer than were on my last birthday cake," she admitted, putting another cupcake on a plate for her daughter. "Did you wash up?" she asked Kylie.

As the little girl scrambled down from the table to do so, Lauryn reminded her, "And don't forget to dry."

"How many candles did you have?" he asked.

Lauryn shook her head. "Not telling."

"Thirty?" he guessed.

She ignored his question and focused on inspecting Kylie's hands when her daughter returned to the table. After Lauryn nodded her approval, Kylie climbed back into her chair and Lauryn struck a match, then set the flame to the wick of his candle.

"Now you hafta make a wish an' blow out the candle," Kylie told him.

"What should I wish for?" he asked her.

"What you want most," she told him, lifting her cupcake to her mouth.

"Hmm." He glanced up at Lauryn. "I might have to give that some thought."

"While you're thinking, wax is melting onto your cupcake," she warned.

He continued to hold her gaze as he let out a puff of air, extinguishing the flame.

"Whad'ya wish?" Kylie asked, her mouth full of cake and icing.

"I wished that you and Zach and your mom would have dinner with me tonight," he confided.

"You're not supposed to tell your wish," Lauryn told him, then admonished her daughter, "And you're not supposed to talk with food in your mouth."

Kylie, still chewing on her cupcake, said nothing.

"Why am I not supposed to tell my wish?" Ryder asked.

"Because then it won't come true," she warned.

He accepted the mug of coffee she set in front of him, stirred in a spoonful of sugar. "Are you really going to deny my birthday wish?"

"You don't have plans to spend your birthday with friends or family?"

"Avery wanted to cook dinner for me, but my mother was supposed to be in town and I didn't want to be part of a dysfunctional family reunion."

"Your mother was planning to come to town for your birthday and you weren't going to spend it with her?"

"Her plans had nothing to do with my birthday," he assured her. "If not for the fact that she always sends me a card and a check, I'd think she didn't even remember the date I was born."

"I'm getting the impression that you're not very close to your mother," she said lightly.

"We're as close as we both want to be."

She frowned at that. "There are times that it feels as if I can't move in this town without tripping over one of my relatives but, at the same time, it's comforting to know that they're never far away if I need them."

"Your family is obviously a little different from mine."

"Still, I'm sure your mother is proud of your success."

He shook his head. "She's never forgiven me for not going to medical school."

"Maybe you don't have an MD, but you do have your own television show," she pointed out.

"My mother doesn't watch television."

She sat down at the table with her own cup of coffee. "Has she seen the billboards proclaiming that you're America's Hottest Handyman?"

"I sincerely hope not," he told her.

"Has she ever actually seen the results of what you do?" she asked curiously.

"She's not impressed—any man can hammer a nail."

"If she met my ex-husband, she'd know that's not true," Lauryn remarked dryly.

Ryder managed a smile at that.

"All done, Mama," Kylie said. "Can I go wash up now?"

They both shifted their attention to the little girl, who had chocolate icing, crumbs and sprinkles smeared on her face and hands.

"No," Lauryn told her. "You sit right there—I'll get a washcloth."

"Are you gonna eat your cupcake?" Kylie asked him, eyeing Ryder's plate hopefully when her mother had left the room.

He might have offered it to her if he wasn't sure his generosity would result in a scolding from Lauryn. "Of course," he told her. "It's my birthday cupcake and extra-special because you made it for me. But there's one sprinkle—" he carefully picked a pink one off the icing "—that's just for you."

He dropped the candy into her outstretched palm and she immediately transferred it to her mouth—and more icing from her hand to her face in the process.

Ryder lifted the cupcake to his mouth to hide his smile.

At that moment, Lauryn came back with a washcloth

to wipe Kylie's face and hands, carefully scrubbing each and every digit on both hands and the spaces in between. "Now you may go play," she said to her daughter when she was done.

Kylie slid off her seat and scampered away.

"That was really sweet," Lauryn said to him. "Sharing your sprinkles with her."

He shrugged. "It wasn't a big deal."

"It was to Kylie," she told him. "And to me."

"It was one sprinkle," he said, uncomfortable with the way she was looking at him—as if there was something special about him because he'd had a two minute conversation with her kid.

Apparently sensing his unease, she shifted the topic of the conversation again. "You were telling me about your mother's visit," she reminded him.

"Just that her intended visit is why I told Avery that I already had plans for tonight."

"You lied to your sister to avoid seeing your mother who didn't end up coming to town, anyway?"

"It wasn't really a lie," he denied. "I did have plans—to stay far away from my mother. So…will you let me take you out for dinner tonight?"

"Actually, my cousin's wife and daughter are coming over tonight. Maura's taking a babysitting certification course and I'm going to take advantage of her services to complete the inventory I left unfinished at the store yesterday."

He studied her for a minute. "I can't figure out if you really have stock to count or if you're brushing me off."

"I really have stock to count," she said, with enough reluctance in her tone to convince him that it was true.

"And if you didn't?" he wondered.

"I still wouldn't go out for dinner with you," she admitted.

"Because you're not attracted to me?" he challenged.

"Because you should be having dinner with the blonde in the red dress."

He didn't expect that she would give a direct answer to his question—and he definitely hadn't expected the answer that she did give. "What blonde in the red dress?"

"The one you were with at Marg & Rita's last week."

"I wasn't *with* her," he denied.

"You left the bar with her."

Damn. He'd hoped no one had seen him slip out the door with Debby, but not for the reasons that Lauryn apparently suspected. "Only to give her a ride home."

"You don't owe me any explanations."

But he wanted to explain. "She's Brody's little sister, who had a little too much to drink in an attempt to forget that she'd recently broken up with her boyfriend. I took her home, saw her safely inside, then went back to my own place because I knew that I had a roofing job to oversee early the next morning."

"You might have told me about the roofing job when I saw you that night," she told him.

He smiled. "I sort of did," he reminded her. "But I'm glad you didn't pick up on my hints or I might have missed seeing you in your...pajamas."

Maura knocked at the door promptly at six o'clock. Though her stepmother, Rachel, was there to supervise, Rachel had asked Lauryn to pretend she wasn't and to give her instructions to the babysitter as if she was on her own. So Lauryn invited Maura inside and showed her the notes she'd left by the phone, with appropriate snack instructions, television guidelines, bedtimes and her cell phone number clearly enumerated.

"An' I gets stowies before bed," Kylie piped up.

"She gets *one* story before bed," Lauryn clarified.

Maura nodded. "What time do you think you'll be home?"

"The inventory shouldn't take more than a couple of hours."

"I need seven more hours for my certification," her niece reminded her.

She smiled at that. "I'm definitely not going to be out *that* long."

"Stay out as long or as short as you need," Rachel told her. "We can come back for more hours another time."

"You play Barbies?" Kylie asked her babysitter.

"I can play whatever you want," Maura told her.

The little girl beamed and skipped off to get her dolls.

"I guess that's everything," Lauryn said, picking up her purse and heading to the door.

"Not quite," Maura said, following her.

"What did I forget?"

The babysitter held out her arms to take the baby.

"Oh, right." Feeling foolish and oddly reluctant, she pressed a kiss to Zachary's forehead and passed him to Maura.

Rachel followed her out the door. "They'll be fine," she promised.

"I know they will," Lauryn agreed.

"I see Andrew finally remembered to come over and replace those weak boards," Rachel noted, looking at the new wood beneath her feet.

"Actually, that was Ryder," Lauryn told her.

"Oh, right—I heard that his crew is doing some work on the house." The other woman's eyes twinkled. "How's that going?"

"I wouldn't know, I'm not allowed to even peek in the kitchen."

"I'm not talking about the kitchen but the man."

"I guess you're a fan of *Ryder to the Rescue*, too?"

"I do like the look of a man in a tool belt," Rachel confirmed. "Why do you think I married your cousin?"

Lauryn sighed. "I wish I'd been half as smart and found a man who was handy around the house—or at least one who knew how to change a toilet paper roll."

"Well, you've got a Mr. Fix-It now."

"I don't have him," she denied.

"Then you're not trying hard enough," her cousin's wife said, followed by an exaggerated wink.

Lauryn shook her head, but she was smiling when she drove away, and feeling incredibly grateful for the support of her often outrageous but always loving family.

Because she was still thinking about Rachel and Maura when she pulled into a parking space in front of The Locker Room, she didn't pay much attention to the pickup that occupied another space. It wasn't until she got out of the van that she spotted the Renovations by Ryder logo on the side—and then saw the man himself leaning against the building near the door.

"I came to help you with inventory," he said, before she had a chance to ask.

"Why?"

"Because we can go for dinner when it's done."

She narrowed her gaze. "I never agreed to that plan."

"I know. And I never suggested the plan because I knew you would think of some reason to shoot it down," he admitted.

He was right, and it irked her that he was right, that he could read her so easily. And, of course, now that he was here, she would feel ridiculous sending him away so that she could complete the task on her own. Instead, she shrugged, "I can't say I understand why you want to spend your birthday counting golf balls, but I'm not going to refuse your help."

"I think you'll figure out the why—" he flashed a quick grin "—eventually."

She slid a key into the lock to release the dead bolt, then stepped inside to disarm the alarm and gestured for him to enter, locking the door again at his back when he'd done so.

"I've inventoried everything in the storeroom," she told him, heading toward the back of the store. "But I haven't had a chance to check what's on the floor. I just need to get the lists from the office."

He followed her lead. She found the documents in the folder where she'd left them, but they weren't exactly as she'd left them.

"Is something wrong?" Ryder asked.

"These are all complete." She noted the initials in the corner of each page. "Somehow Adam got this all done today."

"I think your new manager is bucking for a raise."

She managed a smile. "He knows he'll get one, as soon as I can afford to give it to him."

"Well, I'm glad that was quick, because I'm starving. All I've eaten since breakfast is a cupcake, and that's only thanks to you."

"I've got half a dozen more that I meant to send home with you," she told him.

"We can get them after," he told her, clearly not budging on the dinner idea.

But sharing a meal with him—just the two of them—would really mess with the boundaries she was anxious to maintain. "Look, Ryder," she said, trying to reason with him. "I'm flattered by the attention—as any woman would be—but you can't possibly be interested in me."

"Why can't I be?" he challenged.

She hadn't expected him to make her spell it out, but because she'd been thinking about him—and thinking about all of the reasons she shouldn't be thinking about him—

she had a ready answer. "Because you're Charisma's most famous handyman and heartthrob, and I've got one failed marriage, two kids and a few years on you."

"You're really hung up on the age thing, aren't you?" he mused.

She shook her head. "Out of everything I just said, that's the one fact you focused on?"

"It's the only fact I can't dispute, because you refuse to tell me how old you are," he pointed out. "Aside from that, I think I've figured out a way to prove my interest is real."

"How?" she asked warily.

"Like this," he said, and lowered his head to kiss her.

Chapter Twelve

Lauryn had seen the warning signs.

The way her heart beat just a little bit faster whenever Ryder was near. The way even an accidental touch made her skin tingle. The way his smile made her feel all warm and fluttery inside. But she'd ignored those signs, attributing them to the fact that he was just so darn sexy and it had been so long since she'd felt anything.

Still, she didn't expect that her body would shift from slow burn to full blaze within a second of the first brush of his lips against hers.

Then he lifted his hands to her face, his fingertips trailing gently along the line of her jaw, down her throat. The feather-light touch raised goose bumps on her skin and made everything inside her quiver. He slid a finger beneath her chin, tipping her head back just a little so that he could deepen the kiss.

He coaxed her lips apart, slowly and gently, as if they had all the time in the world and he'd be happy to spend every minute of it kissing her. Then his tongue slid between them to dance with hers—a slow, sensual seduction that made everything inside her tremble and yearn.

She'd never thought a kiss was a big deal. How could she have known when no one had ever kissed her the way that Ryder was kissing her now?

When he finally eased his mouth from hers, they were both breathless.

"Do you still think I'm not interested?" he asked her.

"I can't think at all when you kiss me," she admitted.

He smiled, apparently pleased with her response. "Good," he said, and lowered his head again.

She stepped back, quickly.

Thankfully, he didn't follow, because Lauryn wasn't sure she had the willpower to turn away from him a second time.

"What are you in the mood for?" he asked.

She blinked, uncomprehending. "What?"

His lips curved again in response to her obvious befuddlement. "For dinner," he clarified.

"Oh." She exhaled a slow, unsteady breath and tried to refocus her thoughts.

"Casa Mercado?" he suggested.

She glanced down at her jeans and T-shirt. "I don't think I'm appropriately dressed."

"Valentino's?" he offered as an alternative.

She shook her head. "Too much risk of running into my sister or her husband or someone else in his family who would report back to her."

"Report what?" he asked curiously.

"That I was having dinner with America's Hottest Handyman."

"An event not worthy of any tabloid headlines," he assured her.

"My sisters would disagree."

"Do you have a better suggestion for dinner?"

She considered for a minute, then nodded decisively. "Eli's."

Eli's was famous for juicy cooked-to-order burgers and thick, hand-dipped milk shakes. The atmosphere of the diner-style restaurant, on the other hand, was nothing spectacular. The booths were red vinyl, the tables white Formica, the walls decorated with retro movie posters and all of it was illuminated by bright fluorescent lights.

It certainly wasn't the type of place that Ryder would have chosen to take any woman on a date. On the other hand, he hoped the casual atmosphere would help Lauryn relax in a way he suspected she wouldn't in an establishment with linen tablecloths and a wine list.

She ordered a bacon cheeseburger with curly fries and a vanilla milk shake; he went for the double, also with fries and a chocolate shake.

"Mmm, this is good," she said, after taking the first bite of her burger.

"Anyone ever tell you that you're a cheap date?" he asked teasingly.

"This isn't a date," she said firmly.

He just smiled. "You say to-may-to—"

"I say, this isn't a date," she interjected.

"I invited you to dinner and you, after some bribing and cajoling, agreed. That sounds like a date to me."

Her lips twitched as she fought against a smile. "Are bribing and cajoling part of your usual dating routine?"

"No, I have to admit this is a first for me," he told her. "You're not the first woman to ever say no, but you're the first who's intrigued me enough to want to change the no to a yes." A fact that probably surprised him as much as it surprised her.

He'd been perfectly content with his life. He certainly hadn't been looking for any entanglements. And then Lauryn had opened her front door—with a sweetly smiling child by her side and a chubby-cheeked baby on her hip and all kinds of attitude in her gray-green eyes—and he'd been hooked.

He'd dated all kinds of women—blondes, brunettes and redheads, tall and short, slender and curvy. All that was required was a mutual attraction—and an understanding that there would be no strings, no regrets and definitely no heartache when it was over.

His feelings for Lauryn were different, and he hadn't yet figured out what he was going to do about them. He wasn't looking for love. Truth be told, he wasn't entirely sure he even believed in it. While he couldn't deny that his sister had found something special with her husband, he wasn't certain it would last for a lifetime. He hoped it would—for the sake of Avery and Justin and especially Vanessa—but he wouldn't put any bets on it. Being with Lauryn made him want to gamble on his own future.

"I have two kids," she reminded him.

"You have two wonderful kids," he agreed.

"And Kylie is just starting to get used to her father being gone."

"I'm not trying to take his place," Ryder said, wanting to be clear about that.

"I know that, but Kylie doesn't. She only knows that there's an empty place in her life, and suddenly you're there and you're letting her have pizza and playing Barbies and..."

"And you don't want her to get attached," he finished for her.

"I don't want her to get hurt. Again."

He nodded, because he understood that she had reasons to be cautious. He could even acknowledge that she was smart to want to put on the brakes; he just wasn't convinced that she would succeed. The kiss they'd shared proved the attraction between them was both mutual and intense, and he was looking forward to following wherever it might lead. "I can't change the fact that I'm going to be around a lot over the next couple of months—maybe longer."

She narrowed her gaze. "Why 'maybe longer'?"

"Virginia thinks our viewers might appreciate seeing the results of a more comprehensive project, and she wanted me to discuss the possibility with you."

She took another sip of her milk shake. "What would a more comprehensive project entail?"

"Letting us loose in other rooms of your house," he explained.

"I didn't even want you in my kitchen," she reminded him.

"But it hasn't been so bad, has it?"

"It's only been a week," she pointed out.

"You're right," he admitted. "But Owen doesn't like gaps in the schedule, so he'd probably agree to anything you want."

"Why is there a gap in your schedule?"

"We were originally supposed to head to Georgia to work on the restoration of an antebellum mansion in Watkinsville, but the purchasers have encountered a few snags in their attempts to finalize the paperwork." Having finished his own meal, he stole a fry from her plate. "So what do you think about letting us tackle some more jobs around your house?"

"I'm tempted," she admitted, nudging her plate toward him. "But I'm not sure how I feel about my kids living in a construction zone for an extended period of time."

"That's a valid consideration," he acknowledged. "On the other hand, we're talking about work that you're going to want to have done eventually, and if you have it done now, you won't have to look forward to the noise and debris in the future."

She sighed. "You sure do know how to tempt a girl."

He grinned. "Imagine what I could do if I was actually trying."

Lauryn didn't want to imagine.

She didn't dare let her mind travel too far down the path of any temptation connected to Ryder Wallace. Because more than an hour after they'd left the store—after the kiss—her blood was still humming in her veins.

If he makes you happy, you should go for it.

She didn't know if he made her happy, but there was no doubt he made her yearn. After almost a year and a half of hibernation, her hormones were suddenly wide-awake and clamoring for attention.

Ryder's attention.

Which was precisely why she should thank him for dinner and walk away. Instead, when they left the restaurant she asked, "Did you want to come back to my place to get those cupcakes?"

"Inviting me home after a first date?" he teased.

"It wasn't a date," she said again.

He just grinned.

"And I'm only inviting you to come over to pick up the cupcakes," she further clarified, as much for herself as for him. Besides, Maura and Rachel would be there to chaperone so she didn't have to worry about him trying to steal any more kisses—or her own desire to give them away.

"I'll be right behind you," he promised.

Except that her cousin's wife and daughter stayed only long enough to say hello before they hurried out the door, with Rachel giving her an encouraging wink as she waved goodbye.

Lauryn pulled one of her dining room chairs across the floor, then stood on the seat to reach the top of the hutch where she'd put the box to ensure it was out of reach of her daughter's sweet tooth and eager grasp.

Ryder was immediately behind her. She sucked in a breath as his hands grasped her hips. "What are you doing?"

"Making sure you don't fall."

"I'm not going to fall," she assured him. "I do this all of the time."

"Do you know how many household accidents occur every day because people think any piece of furniture is a ladder?" he asked her.

"No, I don't. How many?"

"I don't know the number offhand," he admitted. "But it's a lot."

"This is sturdy Garrett-made furniture," she told him. "And you can let go of me now."

His eyes, when they lifted to hers, were filled with heat and wicked promise. "Maybe I don't want to."

Her tongue flicked out to moisten her suddenly dry lips. "Do you want your cupcakes to end up on the floor?"

He lifted his hands away, then removed the box from her hands. Lauryn stepped down off the chair.

"Thanks for these," he said.

"Those were to thank you," she reminded him. "And thank you for dinner, too."

"It was my pleasure."

She walked him to the door. "Happy birthday, Ryder."

"Thanks to you and the kids, it was," he said.

And then he kissed her again.

And though she knew kissing him back was a very bad idea, he felt too good to want to stop. In fact, he tasted so good that she wanted to get closer, but there was a box between them. As if he could read her thoughts, he set the container on the table by the door, freeing his hands to touch her. And those strong hands proved to be every bit as talented as his mouth.

Watching him on television, she couldn't help but admire his confident skill as he swung a sledgehammer or taped drywall or nailed trim. Since getting to know him, she'd wondered how it might feel to have his hands stroking over her body, those calloused palms sliding against the soft skin of her breasts, her belly, her thighs. It had been a long time since she'd had a man's hands on her—a long time since she'd wanted a man's hands on her. And when those strong and oh-so-clever hands slid beneath the hem of her T-shirt, his warm touch surpassed every one of her fantasies.

A soft, blissful sigh whispered between her lips. She didn't want him to stop—she didn't ever want him to stop kissing her and touching her. But somewhere in the back of her mind, where a few brain cells were still functioning, she accepted that while getting naked with Ryder might feel really good tonight, she needed to think about tomorrow.

She eased away from him. Breathlessly. Reluctantly. "We can't do this."

"I can't think of a single reason why not," he said.

"For starters, because you're renovating my kitchen."

"The cameras are gone," he pointed out. "There's only you and me here now."

"And my two children," she said, a reminder to herself as much as to Ryder.

"Who are sleeping upstairs."

Upstairs—where her big, empty bed was also located. A bed that would feel a lot less empty with Ryder in it. But as tempting as the idea was, she shook her head. "I don't know how to have an affair."

"Since neither of us is currently involved with anyone else, it wouldn't be an affair," he told her.

"What would it be?"

He smiled, a slow curving of his lips that made her toes curl. "A pleasure." His hands skimmed up her back, raising goose bumps on her flesh and warming the blood in her veins. "A very definite pleasure," he promised.

The way her body was reacting to his touch, she had no doubt that he could fulfill that promise. But she'd never been the type to jump in with both feet, and she had to think about Kylie and Zachary, because everything she did affected her children.

"Don't you think that giving in to this…attraction would complicate our business arrangement?"

"It's already complicated," he told her.

"And getting involved would complicate it even further."

"Maybe," he acknowledged. "Or maybe it would alleviate some of the tension between us."

And there was no doubt she was feeling...tense. But she had to be smart.

"I want you, Lauryn. I didn't want to want you," he admitted. "But I've given up denying that I do."

"Ryder—" He touched a finger to her lips, silencing her so that he could continue.

"I want to strip you naked and make love to you." His voice was as seductive as a caress, the words sliding over her skin like a lover's touch. "But we'll wait until you're sure that it's what you want, too."

"You might be waiting a long time," she warned.

His lips curved again in a smile that was slow and sexy and just a little bit smug. "I don't think so."

"Good night, Ryder," she said firmly.

"Good night, Lauryn." He brushed his lips over hers once more. "Sweet dreams."

After a rain delay in Martinsville necessitated postponing Sunday's scheduled race, Tristyn finally returned to Charisma on Tuesday. Lauryn was in the store when her sister came in, her arms full of bags of Halloween decorations. She tried to protest that they were a sporting goods store and no one cared if there weren't any pumpkins or ghosts on display, but Tristyn waved off her arguments and got busy transforming the front window mannequins into zombies—albeit zombies wearing high-end sporting apparel and top-of-the-line athletic shoes.

When Adam came in at noon—because Lauryn opened the store on Tuesdays, Wednesdays and Thursdays—she was finally able to escape from her position at the front register.

"I need to talk to you about something," she said to

Tristyn when she found her sister arranging fake cobwebs and creepy plastic spiders on a skateboard display.

Her sister set another spider in place, then turned to face her. "You didn't forget to cancel the order for those ski jackets, did you?"

"No, I canceled the order. This has nothing to do with the inventory. Well, maybe it does. Indirectly."

"You're flustered," Tristyn mused. "And you never get flustered."

"I kissed Ryder." She blurted the words out like a confession. "Or he kissed me. But then I kissed him back."

Her sister's lips curved. "I think I understand now why you're flustered. This is certainly an interesting—if not unexpected—development."

"No, it's *not* interesting," Lauryn denied. "It's…crazy and irresponsible and reckless and dangerous and crazy—"

"You said 'crazy' twice," Tristyn pointed out.

"Because it needs to be said twice. Maybe even three times or ten times. Because I never should have let it happen and it's all Jordyn's fault."

"How is it Jordyn's fault?" her sister wanted to know. "And why are you assigning blame? Unless he's a really lousy kisser, and if he is, I don't want to know—it will ruin all of my fantasies."

"Of course, he isn't a lousy kisser. He's at the complete opposite end of the spectrum of kissers. And it's Jordyn's fault because she told me to make the cupcakes."

"You made cupcakes for his birthday?" Tristyn queried.

Lauryn frowned at that. "How did you know it was his birthday?"

"There were about a thousand 'happy birthday' messages to him on Twitter."

"You follow him on Twitter?"

"Half a million people follow him on Twitter," her sister said matter-of-factly.

"Well, I'm not on Twitter and I didn't know it was his birthday," Lauryn said. "The cupcakes were supposed to be a thank-you because he stayed to watch the kids on Friday when Jordyn abandoned them."

Tristyn waved away her explanation as if it was inconsequential. "Tell me about the kiss."

Just the memory of the kiss had heat flooding through her body, warming her from the top of her head to the toes curling inside of her shoes. "I can't remember the last time I was kissed like that," she admitted. "If ever. It was… pretty much perfect."

Her sister sighed dreamily. "I suspected that about him. He has the aura of a man who knows what he's doing in all aspects of his life."

"He knows what he's doing," she confirmed.

"What happened after the kiss?" Tristyn asked.

"We went out for dinner. To Eli's."

Her sister was clearly unimpressed. "He kissed you senseless and then bought you a burger?"

"Eli's was my choice."

Tristyn sighed. "Sometimes I can't believe we're sisters."

"We had a good time," she said, just a little defensively.

"You had milk shakes under fluorescent lights when you deserve wine and candlelight."

"We had a good time," she repeated. Then she thought about the kiss again—the kiss she hadn't been able to stop thinking about—and mentally amended "good" to "great."

"I'm not disputing that you probably did," Tristyn told her. "I just think you should expect more. You deserve more."

"Maybe I should consider one of those Rabbits you were talking about."

Her sister shook her head. "A battery-operated device is no substitute for a flesh-and-blood man, especially not when that man is Ryder Wallace."

She didn't disagree, but there were still a lot of reasons to be wary. "He's six years younger than me."

"So?"

"So I'm looking ahead at forty and he's not even thirty."

"You're thirty-four," her sister noted. "Forty is a long way off."

"Maybe, but I still graduated from college before he'd finished high school."

"So?" Tristyn said again.

She sighed and finally confided her biggest concern. "I have to think about my children—especially Kylie."

"Of course, you have to think about the children," her sister agreed. "But you need to think about yourself, too. What do *you* want? Are you looking for a fling or a relationship?"

"I wasn't looking for anything," she denied. "Not until he kissed me."

"And now?" Tristyn prompted.

"Now—" She blew out a frustrated breath. "Now I can't seem to think about anything but how much I want him naked and in my bed."

"An admirable goal," her sister assured her.

"I thought you would be the voice of reason, that you would point out all of the reasons that even thinking about getting naked with him is a bad idea."

"No, you didn't," Tristyn said. "If you really wanted to be talked out of this, you'd be talking to Jordyn."

"Except that Jordyn advised me to 'go for it.'"

"Obviously falling in love again has changed her perspective on life. And maybe that should be a lesson to you."

Lauryn shook her head. "I can't afford to make any more mistakes in my life."

"Relationships are always a risk," Tristyn acknowledged. "If you don't put your heart on the line you can't lose. On the other hand, you can't win, either."

Chapter Thirteen

Ryder was pleased with the progress his crew was making on Lauryn's kitchen—and frustrated that he'd made absolutely zero progress with the woman herself. He thought they'd had a good time together on his birthday. They'd talked and laughed and shared a couple of sizzling kisses. But in the almost two weeks that had passed since then, he'd barely seen her—and he never had an opportunity to be alone with her.

He really wanted to be alone with her. He wanted to kiss her and touch her and—

And there she was. Once again on her way out the door when he was coming in. But this time, he changed direction, falling into step beside her as she headed out with Zachary in his stroller and Kylie by her side. The backpack on the little girl told him that she was on her way to meet the school bus, which picked her up at the bottom of the driveway every morning.

"What have you got stuffed into that pack today?" Ryder asked Kylie.

"My Halloween costume," she told him. "We're havin' a party at school an' I'm gonna be a pwincess."

"I bet you'll be the prettiest princess in the whole school," he told her.

"You wanna come to my party?" she asked.

"As much fun as I'm sure that would be, I think your mom would prefer if I stayed here and worked on her kitchen."

"Definitely," Lauryn agreed.

Kylie tipped her head back to look at her mother. "Are you comin' to my party?"

"Yes, I'll be there," she confirmed.

"You hafta bwing tweats," the little girl reminded her.

"Mrs. Shea knows that I'm bringing a fruit tray," Lauryn told her as the school bus pulled up.

"'Kay," Kylie said. She quickly hugged her mom, then Ryder, then she leaned in to kiss her brother's cheek before she tackled the big stairs leading onto the bus.

"There's one Garrett female who isn't stingy with her affection," Ryder noted as the bus doors closed, swallowing the little girl up inside.

"Schulte," her mother corrected automatically.

He shook his head. "That might be her name, but the blood in her veins is pure Garrett."

Lauryn's lips curved just a little, as if she was pleased by the thought, but all she said was, "Aren't you supposed to be working on my kitchen?"

"The work will get done," he promised. "And I want to know why you've been dodging me for the last couple of weeks."

"I haven't been dodging you," she denied, pivoting the stroller around and heading back up the driveway. "I've seen you almost every day."

"But you're careful never to be alone with me."

She lifted Zachary out of the stroller and put him in his car seat, while Ryder collapsed the stroller for her and set it in the back of the van. "There's no reason for me to be alone with you."

"I didn't mean to scare you off," he said, when he had her full attention again.

"You didn't." But she was looking at her car keys when she said it.

He tipped her chin up, forcing her to meet his gaze. "Prove it," he said. "Have dinner with me tonight."

"Tonight is Halloween," she reminded him.

"You don't eat on Halloween?"

Her lips curved. "Usually only chocolate bars and gummy bears."

"After trick-or-treating," he guessed.

She nodded.

"Can I come along?"

"Only if you don't expect me to share the candy."

"You can have all of it, but—" he winked at her "—I have dibs on your kisses."

I have dibs on your kisses.

His words continued to echo in the back of Lauryn's mind throughout the day—while she was at the store, while she was assembling the fruit tray in her mother's kitchen, even while she was at the Halloween party at Kylie's preschool. Because she knew he wasn't talking about candy kisses, and she would gladly trade away every last gummy bear to feel his lips on hers again.

But she wanted more than his kisses. She wanted *him.* And that was why she'd been dodging him. Not that staying away from him had stopped the wanting, so when he'd asked if he could join them for trick-or-treating, she didn't see any point in denying his request.

When the doorbell rang, Lauryn was struggling to get Zachary into the pumpkin costume his sister had worn a few years earlier. Of course, Kylie had been two months younger—and about five pounds lighter—on her first Halloween.

After instructing Kylie to look out the window to ensure it was Ryder at the door, Lauryn gave her daughter permission to let him in.

"Hi, Wyder!" Kylie greeted him.

He took in her costume and immediately offered a deep, courtly bow. "Good evening, Your Highness."

She giggled. "You like my costume?"

"Very much," he told her. "But...I think you're missing something."

Her hands immediately went to the top of her head to ensure that her sparkly crown was in place. "What's missin'?"

"A trick-or-treat bag. Something worthy of a princess." He held up the one he carried—made of white satin fabric and decorated with ribbons and sparkly beads with a lace drawstring.

Kylie gasped, her eyes wide. "Is that for me?"

Ryder nodded. "Thank you!" she said, and threw herself into his arms.

He caught her as best he could, considering that his hands were full, and hugged her back. "You're welcome."

She accepted the bag and peered inside. "Look, Mama—there's even candy inside."

"You just made her day," Lauryn said, when Kylie had skipped away. "That's quite an improvement over a reusable grocery bag."

"I brought something for you, too," he said, offering her a bottle of wine. "The clerk assured me that nothing goes better with gummy bears than a nice merlot."

"I find a cool, crisp chardonnay really brings out the flavor of the green ones."

He lifted a brow. "You separate out the colors as you eat them?"

"Doesn't everyone?"

He chuckled. "No." He moved toward the refrigerator with a grocery bag in hand. "I also brought a couple of steaks and baking potatoes that we can throw on the grill later."

Kyle returned with sparkly shoes now on her feet. "Can we go, Mama?" she asked. "Is it time?"

"I think somebody's getting anxious," Ryder told her.

"She's been asking the same question since we got home from the school party," Lauryn told him.

"Are you comin' twick-or-tweatin' wif us, Wyder?"

"Yes, I am," he said.

"But you're not dwessed up."

He feigned shock. "You don't recognize my costume?" She shook her head.

"I'm Ryder to the Rescue," he said with a dramatic flourish, making her giggle. "I save home owners from leaky pipes and crumbling plaster. And sometimes I even take princesses door-to-door on Halloween night."

Lauryn boosted Zachary onto her hip. "Let's go, princess and Ryder to the Rescue, before this pumpkin turns into a grumpy bear."

It was nice to have company on the outing. Lauryn particularly appreciated a second set of adult eyes watching over Kylie as there were always so many people milling about—many of them unrecognizable in their costumes—that she worried about losing sight of her daughter. At least she didn't have to be concerned about Zachary, who was content—at least this year—to ride along in his stroller.

"Did you make her costume?" Ryder asked when they were stopped at the end of a driveway watching Kylie make her way to the front door. "It looks like a real dress."

"It was Maura's flower girl dress when her dad married Rachel." She smiled at the memory. "Of course, she was eight at the time, so I had to take in the sides and chop several inches off the hem. But after that, I just sewed on a lot of sparkling beads and stuff to make it look more princess-y."

"You did a great job."

"Thanks, but I was actually hoping she'd want to be

something more traditional—like a black cat or a ghost," she admitted.

"What's wrong with her being a princess?" he asked.

Lauryn shrugged. "I'm just worried that I'm not doing her any favors by perpetuating her illusions about fairy tales and happy endings."

"She's three," he reminded her. "She should believe in happy endings."

"Maybe," she said dubiously.

"Just because your Prince Charming turned out to be a frog is no reason to undermine her beliefs," he chided gently.

"Is that what you think I'm doing?" she asked, frowning as she realized he might be right.

"I don't know—is it?"

She sighed. "Maybe."

"And maybe your Prince Charming wasn't really a prince but the big bad wolf in disguise," he suggested.

"Now you're mixing up your fairy tales," she told him.

"My point is that you should have faith that the real Prince Charming is somewhere in your future. Or maybe even—" he slung an arm across her shoulders "—in your present."

She tipped her head back to look at him. "I always thought Prince Charming would wear a crown."

"That's only in the storybooks—in real life, he sometimes wears a tool belt."

When they had headed out at six thirty, Kylie had skipped down the driveway with an empty trick-or-treat bag and a heart full of excitement and enthusiasm. It wasn't even seven thirty when Kylie opened her bag to show her mother the contents. "Look, Mama, it's almost fulled up."

"Already? That's great."

"You're only saying that because you want to go home,"

Ryder guessed, speaking in a low tone so that only Lauryn could hear.

"I would like to get Zachary into bed at his usual time," she acknowledged.

"I can stay out with Kylie if you want to take him home," Ryder offered.

"That's not necessary," she said, watching as Kylie made her way up the flagstone walk of the next house. "Her energy will fade before much longer."

"That's something I have yet to see," he noted.

Lauryn smiled. "You will tonight. She'll go full speed ahead right up to the moment that she crashes."

Which was exactly what she did a short while later. They were three blocks from home when Kylie suddenly seemed to droop at her mother's feet, her bag of candy falling to the sidewalk. "I tired, Mama. You ca-wy me?"

Lauryn had no objections to carrying her daughter from the living room to her bed when she fell asleep downstairs—or even from the van into the house—but three blocks was another matter.

"Why don't you stand on the back of Zachary's stroller?" she suggested as an alternative.

Kylie shook her head. "My feets hurt."

"This sounds like a job for Ryder to the Rescue," he interjected, swooping down and lifting her high in the air to settle her on his shoulders.

The little girl screeched with terrified glee and grabbed hold of his hair so that it stood up in little tufts where her fingers grasped it. The scream had given Lauryn's heart a jolt—her daughter's precarious position jolted it again. She opened her mouth to demand that Ryder put Kylie down, then she saw the breathless smile on Kylie's face and the words stuck in her throat.

Lauryn couldn't begin to count the number of times she'd been carried like that on her father's shoulders when she was a child. It had been the perfect vantage point to watch the Fourth of July parade on Main Street or to look at the newly hatched baby birds in a nest in their backyard, and it was her favorite way to be carried when her own legs had been too tired to walk any farther.

The memories flooded back to her as she watched Ryder with her daughter, and something deep inside of her opened up, like a flower blooming in response to the warmth of the sun.

And that was before Kylie rested her chin on top of Ryder's head and said, "This was the bestest Halloween ever."

Ryder had just poured the wine when Kylie came back downstairs after her bath. Her costume was gone, but she was wearing a princess nightgown with fuzzy slippers on her feet.

"She wanted to say good-night," Lauryn explained.

"Of course," he said. Then to Kylie, he said, "Good night, princess."

She smiled shyly. "Kiss?"

He kissed her puckered lips.

"Will you come twick-or-tweatin' wif me again next year?" she asked softly.

Over the years, he'd been invited to countless events by numerous women, but he was certain he'd never received a more beguiling invitation. He nodded without hesitation. "It's a date."

She smiled again. "Night night, Wyder."

Lauryn took her hand and led her daughter up to bed. When she came back a few minutes later, it was with a worried expression on her face.

"I wish you hadn't done that," she said to him.

"What did I do?"

"You told Kylie that you'd go trick-or-treating with her next year."

"I don't see the problem," he admitted.

She folded her arms across her chest. "She might only be three and a half, but she's already had enough experience with disappointment in her life."

"I have no intention of disappointing your daughter," he assured her.

"Next Halloween is a whole year away," she pointed out. "You probably don't even know where you'll be next October."

He nodded his head in acknowledgment of the fact. "That's true."

"And when you're not here, Kylie will be left wondering what she did wrong."

"Wherever I might be, I'm sure I can come back to take her trick-or-treating," he said reasonably. "And if I can't, I'll at least talk to her and let her know why."

"Assuming that, twelve months from now, you remember an offhand promise that you made to a little girl."

He unfolded her arms and linked their hands together. "I'll remember, Lauryn."

But the furrow in her brow remained.

"Are you really worried that I'm going to disappoint Kylie?" he wondered aloud. "Or are you worried that I'll disappoint you?"

Her eyes flashed with something that might have been anger—or guilt. "I don't worry about being disappointed anymore. I expect it."

"Is that why you're trying to piss me off?" he asked quietly. "So that I'll get mad and leave, and your disappointment will be justified?"

"I'm not trying to do any such thing," she denied, then she sighed wearily. "Or maybe I am. I don't know—this whole situation is outside my realm of experience."

He dropped a brief but firm kiss on her lips before he released her hands. "The only place I'm going right now is to fire up the grill to cook the steaks, because man—and woman—cannot live on gummy bears alone."

"We also have fun-sized chocolate bars and marshmallow ghosts," she reminded him.

"Those will be for dessert."

So they ate steaks and baked potatoes, washing both down with the excellent merlot he'd brought over. Sitting across from Ryder, Lauryn found herself replaying their earlier conversation and wondering why she was continuing to deny what she wanted. Did she expect him to disappoint her? Or was she more worried that she might disappoint him?

She'd only had one lover in the past eight years, and only one lover prior to that. And in each of those situations, she'd been in love with the man before she'd made love with him. She'd never had a fling.

She wasn't in love with Ryder, but she was definitely in lust. She wanted him with an intensity that bordered on desperation—and that was definitely something she hadn't experienced before. But she still didn't know if she had the courage to follow her sisters' advice and "go for it."

"I think Kylie was right," Lauryn said, setting her fork and knife on her empty plate. "This was a really good Halloween."

"Actually, she said it was the bestest," he reminded her.

"Well, at three and a half, she hasn't experienced many Halloweens." She nudged a bowl of candy toward him. "Gummy bear?"

He peered inside. "You ate all of the red ones."

"And left all of the green ones for you."

"I'm in the mood for something sweeter," he said, edging his chair closer to hers.

He captured her mouth slowly, but it was indeed a capture. She had no hope of evading—and no desire to even try. She savored his kiss—the warmth, the texture, the flavor. She'd never known a kiss could be so much and make her want so much more.

As his mouth moved over hers, patiently, seductively, her mind clouded and her body yearned. Yes, what she was feeling was definitely lust. And maybe just a little bit more.

"I'll load up these dishes and take them downstairs for you," he said when he ended the kiss.

It frustrated her that he could switch gears so effortlessly while her body continued to battle with her brain.

"Why do you do that?" she asked when he came back, the frustration in her voice mirroring that of her body.

"Do what?" he asked, a little warily.

"Get me all stirred up and then walk away."

"You said you needed some time," he reminded her, sliding his chair back into place at the table. "I'm trying to give it to you."

She should be grateful for that, but right now she was feeling too turned-on to appreciate his restraint. "I haven't had sex in a year and a half," she admitted. "That's probably enough time."

His fingers tightened on the chair. "Are you saying that if I were to make a move, you wouldn't object?"

She shook her head and moved closer to him, sliding her hands up his chest to link behind his head. "I'm tired of waiting for you to make a move."

And then *she* kissed *him*.

Ryder thought he was pretty good at reading her, but Lauryn definitely surprised him when she moved forward to press her lips to his. Her mouth was soft and cool and just a little bit uncertain—as if she wasn't quite sure how he would respond.

He responded by sliding his arms around her and drawing her closer. Her body swayed into his, her soft womanly curves pressing against him and causing all of the blood in his head to quickly migrate south. But he held his own desire in check, letting her set the tone and the pace of the kiss.

One hand slid off his shoulder to trail down his arm until her hand caught his. She linked their fingers together as she eased her lips from his, then turned and led him toward the stairs.

He followed her willingly. Happily. Eagerly.

She paused at the door of her bedroom. "I should—"

"Check on the kids," he guessed.

She nodded.

"I'll wait right here," he promised, because he understood that she was, first and foremost, a mother. And surprisingly, he didn't find that aspect of her life off-putting at all.

She didn't make him wait long, but he could tell by the uncertainty in her eyes when she returned that those few moments she was away had been sufficient to create doubts about the next step. He was confident that he could erase all of those doubts in thirty seconds if he put his hands on her, but it needed to be her decision, so he held his ground.

"They're both sleeping," she told him.

"They had a lot of excitement today."

"It was a great day," she said, "but I'm still not convinced it was the bestest Halloween ever."

He recognized a challenge when it was issued. "I bet I could convince you."

"I'm willing to let you give it your best shot," she said.

It was all the invitation he needed.

He lifted her off her feet and carried her across the threshold into her bedroom.

Chapter Fourteen

Lauryn's breath whooshed out of her lungs; her heart fluttered wildly inside her chest. She'd watched many movie heroes carry their lovers off into the sunset, but she'd never imagined that it would happen to her. The fact that the sun had set hours earlier didn't detract at all from the sheer romance of the moment when Ryder swept her into his arms.

A thin sliver of moonlight slanted into the room, guiding him toward the bed, where he set her back on her feet and kissed her again.

Nerves jumped in her belly, twisted into knots. Now that they were here, she expected a race toward the finish line. And that was okay—her body was more than ready for the intimate connection they both craved. But she was apprehensive, too. Eighteen months was a long time and she wanted this—wanted *him*—so much she was a little worried that the anticipation might supersede the main event.

Then his hands moved over her as he deepened the kiss, and she stopped worrying. He found the buttons at the front of her shirt, his fingers adeptly unfastening them. It was only when he parted the fabric and she felt a rush of cool air against her skin that she remembered she had a plan for this eventuality.

"Wait."

He paused with his hands at the button of her jeans. "What am I waiting for?"

"I need a minute to change into something…"

"More comfortable?" he guessed.

"More seductive," she admitted.

"*You* are seductive enough," he told her.

"I can do better," she promised.

"Naked would be better."

She pressed a brief kiss to his lips. "I just need one minute."

"One minute," he agreed.

She opened her top drawer and pulled out the black silk slip with lace inserts that she'd recently bought in anticipation of showing it to Ryder, even before she was sure that she would ever do so. She ducked into the bathroom and quickly stripped away her clothes, spritzed some of her favorite but rarely used fragrance on her skin, then slipped into the silk. The fabric was cool against her body, making her nipples tighten, and the hem flirted with the tops of her thighs. Drawing in a long, deep breath for courage, she opened the door.

Ryder had turned on the lamp beside the bed and was lounging on top of the covers, staring at his watch, when she stepped back into the bedroom. Though she didn't say anything, he immediately looked up, as if he somehow sensed her presence. Then he rose from the bed, his eyes skimming over her from her head to her toes with obvious appreciation. "Wow."

She smiled, the single word successfully untangling most of the knots in her belly. "I told you I'd only be a minute."

"You were actually behind that closed door for almost a minute and a half."

"You were keeping track?"

"It felt like the longest eighty-five seconds of my life—but you are definitely worth the wait." He took her hands to draw her closer and felt her fingers tremble. "Are you nervous?"

"A little," she admitted. "It's been a long time for me."

"There's nothing to be afraid of," he promised.

"Should we talk first?"

"If you wanted to talk, you should have said so before you came out of the bathroom wearing nothing but…that."

"I just wanted to reassure you that I have no expectations beyond tonight," she said.

"I might not be the forever-after type, but I don't do one-night stands anymore, either," he told her. "So why don't we agree to simply enjoy being together for so long as we do?"

"One day at a time?"

"Something like that," he agreed.

"That works for me," she said.

"Good. Are we done talking now?"

He didn't give her a chance to answer before he covered her lips in a slow, deep kiss that had all of her worries fading away like a bad dream. He had a way of kissing her that made her feel not just wanted but adored, not just desired but cherished.

She tugged his T-shirt out of his jeans so that her hands could explore beneath it. Her palms slid over the warm, taut skin of his stomach, slowly tracing each rippling contour. He took his hands off her only long enough to lift his shirt over his head and toss it aside, allowing her to continue her exploration of his glorious muscles unimpeded.

And his muscles were indeed glorious. As tantalizing as he'd appeared in all those close-ups on TV, the images didn't do justice to him. She pressed her mouth to the warm skin, just above his heart that was beating as rapidly as her own.

He took a minute to shed most of his clothes, with the exception of a pair of very sexy black boxer-style briefs, then he laid her down on top of the bed and straddled her thighs. His fingers caught the edge of her slip and began to slide it upward over her skin.

She grabbed his wrists. "What are you doing?"

"As fabulous as this looks on you, I want it off—I want to see *you*."

"No, you don't."

"Yes, I do," he insisted.

She shook her head. "Ryder, I've given birth to two children—"

"Two beautiful children," he agreed. "Why would you think that carrying them would somehow make you any less beautiful?"

How was it that he always seemed to know exactly what to say? It was unnerving…and incredibly appealing. But she'd lived with her own doubts and insecurities too long to give them up easily now. "I thought guys your age were only interested in perfect bodies."

"And I thought women your age were more comfortable in their own skin," he countered, his hands continuing to explore her body in a way that assured her even more than his words that he wasn't finding any flaws.

"Touché," she said. "But you still don't know how old I am."

"Thirty-three," he guessed.

She frowned. "Where did you come up with that number?"

"I figured you did four years of college to get your business degree, then another two for your master's. If you started college at eighteen, then you would have been twenty-four when you finished, and Tristyn mentioned that you worked at Garrett Furniture for four years after you graduated and before you got married, and you were married for five and a half years." He looked at her. "Am I close?"

"Actually, I turned thirty-four on my last birthday." She eyed him warily. "It doesn't bother you that I'm six years older than you?"

"No," he said. "I just wish it didn't bother you that I'm six years younger than you."

"I'm trying not to think about it."

"Let me help you not think," he suggested, lowering his head to kiss her again.

"Okay," she said. "But the slip is not coming off."

"If you really want to keep it on, I won't object…this time."

Despite his opposition to the silk covering her body, it didn't seem to get in his way or inhibit his exploration of her body—or her enjoyment. He brushed his thumbs over her nipples, already tightly beaded beneath the silk, the brief contact making her gasp as arrows of pleasure streaked toward her core. Then he lowered his head and suckled her through the fabric until she was panting and squirming and desperately wishing that his mouth was on her bare flesh.

Thankfully, he had no inhibitions about his own body. And why would he? He was hard and strong and so perfectly put together he might have been sculpted by a master. But he wasn't a monument of cold, hard marble—he was a man, warm and strong. And he was in her bed. All those yummy muscles were right there for her to explore with her hands and lips and body.

His hands slid beneath the fabric, his fingertips trailing along the sensitive skin on the inside of her thighs, gently urging them apart. When he parted the soft folds of skin at the apex of her thighs, he hummed his approval.

Not quite brave enough to slide her hand beneath the waistband of his boxers, she explored the size and shape of him through the fabric.

She bit down on her lip when his hands slid between her thighs again. Keeping his gaze focused on her face, he dallied beneath the hem of her slip. When his thumb grazed the aching nub at her center, the light touch set off a myriad of sensations that made her gasp with shock and pleasure.

"I think I found a sensitive spot," he teased, brushing his thumb over it again.

"Ryder…*please*."

He slid a finger deep inside of her and slowly withdrew it. She clenched her teeth together to prevent herself from making any sound as he repeated the action, with two fingers this time. Then his thumb found that ultrasensitive spot again and circled around it. Her breath caught in her lungs as everything inside her tensed and tightened…and… finally…shattered.

He captured her mouth with his, swallowing the cries she could no longer hold back and holding her close while the aftershocks continued to shudder through her body.

"Definitely a sensitive spot," he mused, smiling against her mouth.

"I told you it's been a really long time for me," she said, her tone accusing.

"So you did," he acknowledged. "And I wanted to make sure the experience was enjoyable for you."

"Do you have any doubts?"

He grinned as he discarded his boxers. "Not one. And we're not close to being done yet."

"Condom," she said, suddenly remembering the box she'd bought *just in case*. "In the night table drawer."

"I've already got that covered," he said. "Or I will in a second."

It took a little longer than that, but once he'd ensured her protection, he parted her thighs with his knees and, in one smooth, powerful stroke, buried himself inside of her. She closed her eyes and sighed her appreciation. He was so hard and so deep…and it felt so good.

Then he began to move, thrusting deep, deeper, and sending fresh waves of pleasure straight to her core. She wrapped her arms and legs around him, anchoring herself to him as wave after wave of sensation washed over her. She tried to hold on, but it was too much. So she gave herself over to the storm and let it carry her away, and finally Ryder let himself sink into the abyss with her.

* * *

It was a long time later before her breathing evened out. Minutes? Hours? Days? She didn't know; she didn't care. She felt too completely sated to worry about anything.

Several more minutes passed after that before Ryder eased himself off her and brushed her hair away from her face. "You were...wow."

She shook her head. "The wow was all your doing."

"Or maybe the wow was the two of us together," he suggested, wrapping his arm around her and pulling her against his body.

She smiled as she laid her head on his shoulder and her palm on his chest, beneath which she could feel the still-rapid beating of his heart. "I'm convinced," she told him. "This was definitely the bestest Halloween ever."

"For me, too."

He continued just to hold her for a long time, his hand stroking leisurely down her back. She felt comfortable and contented and was starting to drift off to sleep when reality jolted her awake again.

She lifted her head to look at him. "You can't stay."

"I know," he admitted.

"I wish you could, but—"

"You don't have to explain," he told her. "I understand."

He eased himself into a sitting position, then brought her mouth to his and kissed her, long and slow and deep.

When he finally pulled away and reached for his shirt, she glanced at the clock. "You know, it really isn't that late," she decided.

He paused, one arm in a sleeve. "There are still a lot of hours before sunrise," he agreed.

"So you can stay a little longer, if you want."

The shirt dropped back to the floor.

"I want," he said, and proceeded to show her how much.

* * *

When Lauryn arrived home the next day and saw Ryder's truck still in her driveway, her heart did a happy dance inside her chest. While the rational part of her brain warned that she was venturing into dangerous territory, she didn't care. All that mattered was that he was there.

And when she finally got the kids into the house and he smiled at her, the intensity of his gaze made her suspect that he'd been thinking about her as much as she'd been thinking about him throughout the day.

"I missed you," he told her.

The simple sincerity of the words filled her heart, but she kept her own tone casual and light when she said, "I would have hoped you'd be too busy finishing my kitchen to miss me."

"We finished at two," he told her. "The unveiling is tomorrow morning, if you can be here."

She would have to call Adam to open the store for her, but she didn't want to wait a minute longer than necessary to see her new kitchen. "I *will* be here," she promised.

"Good."

"What's in the microwave?" she asked, when she heard the appliance ding.

"Pasta sauce."

"You're making dinner again?"

"Last night I grilled," he said, as if that didn't count. "And this is just spaghetti."

But it wasn't "just" anything to Lauryn. Finding a handsome man in her ad hoc kitchen, making dinner for her family, was a big deal to her. And it made her question again the wisdom of what she was doing.

Could she really have a physical relationship with him— and the greatest sex she'd ever imagined—and not expect it to develop into something more? After one night, it was already more. Because even more than she enjoyed being with him, she loved how comfortable and natural he was with Kylie and Zachary. Not surprisingly, her children were both becoming more attached to Ryder every day, and maybe that should have been the biggest warning sign—her signal to back off. But she knew it was already too late for that, and she was already more than halfway in love with him.

Her sisters had encouraged her to have a fling—and she hadn't been looking for anything more than that. But Ryder tempted her to want more. A lot more. And though it was undoubtedly foolish to be falling for another man only weeks after her divorce was finalized, she couldn't deny that she was.

He stirred the pasta, peeked into the living room to make sure the kids were otherwise occupied, then tugged Lauryn out of sight to put his arms around her. "I've been thinking about kissing you all day."

"I've been thinking about that, too—and all of the other fun things that go along with kissing," she admitted.

He slid his hands up her back and slowly down again. "Does that mean I might get an invitation to stay late tonight?"

"You can stay as late as you want," she promised.

Since Tristyn and Jordyn had been part of the introductory segment, Lauryn invited them back for the unveiling. Over the past five weeks, Kylie had become accustomed to the presence of Ryder's crew and the cameras, and so both children would be with her when she entered their new kitchen for the first time.

She'd watched countless episodes of *Ryder to the Rescue* since the project started and never failed to be impressed by the transformations effected by his crew. There was absolutely no reason to be nervous, but she couldn't deny that she was.

Ryder went through his usual introductory spiel before he turned to face Lauryn. "Are you ready for this?"

She nodded.

"Are you excited or apprehensive?" he asked.

"A little of both," she admitted.

"Then let's not keep you in suspense any longer," he said, gesturing for Stan to open the door.

"Oh." Her eyes went wide and almost immediately filled with tears. "Wow."

She stepped into the center of the room and slowly turned in a circle so that she could take in the view from all angles. "It doesn't even look like the same room."

Ryder smiled. "Wasn't that the idea?"

"It was," she agreed. "I just never expected anything like this."

"You picked the white shaker-style cabinets, the charcoal granite countertops, glass-and-polished-stone-mosaic backsplash and graphite ceramic floor tiles, even the stainless steel hardware," he reminded her.

There were also brand-new stainless steel appliances, including a countertop range, chimney-style range hood, double wall ovens, French door refrigerator and dishwasher.

"You've got the island you wanted, with lots of extra storage and pendant lights over the breakfast bar. The sink has been moved to the short wall, so you've got a lot more usable counter space. And instead of a single window looking into the backyard, you now have a whole wall of windows, which will let in tons of natural light and allow you to keep an eye on the kids when they're out there."

"Everything is...perfect."

"But there's one more little surprise," Ryder said, opening the double doors of a pantry-style cupboard with pull-out drawers.

Lauryn stepped closer, already loving the drawers that would make all of the space so much more accessible. Then she saw that the drawer was already stocked with baking supplies—different kinds of flours and sugars and more. The next drawer held baking trays, measuring cups and utensils—and her cookie cutters, neatly organized in clear stackable containers so that she could see what was inside.

The whole kitchen was amazing, but this cupboard showed her more clearly than anything else that Ryder really knew her. And despite the public unveiling, she understood that this was his personal gift to her.

"When you were packing up your old kitchen, you mentioned that you wished you had time to do more of the baking you used to enjoy. Unfortunately, we couldn't put more hours into your days, but we wanted to ensure that everything was available for you whenever you might find the time."

Conscious of the cameras that were rolling, she blinked back the tears. "This is so much more than I ever expected," she said. "I don't think there's any way that I could ever thank you and your crew enough."

She heard a voice—she thought maybe it was Brody's—pipe up from the background. "You could start by baking us some cookies."

Lauryn laughed as she wiped an errant tear from her cheek. "I'll be baking this weekend," she promised.

While Ryder said a final few words for the benefit of his television viewers, she gestured for Tristyn and Jordyn to come in to check out the space.

After they'd opened all of the cupboards and drawers, her sisters flanked her by the island. "Does this mean we're forgiven?" Jordyn asked.

"You think I'm going to forget that you forged my signature on the application just because I have a fabulous new kitchen?"

"How about the fact that you have a fabulous new man?" Tristyn suggested.

"That's more likely," she acknowledged.

"So…things are good between you and the hunky handyman?" Jordyn prompted.

She was helpless to prevent the smile that curved her lips. "Things are very good."

Tristyn had started to say something else when her cell phone chimed. She pulled it out of her pocket, then cursed softly beneath her breath. "Shoot, I've gotta run—no sharing any details until Saturday."

"What's Saturday?"

"Spa day," Jordyn answered, because Tristyn had already gone.

"I can't make this Saturday," Lauryn told her.

"Why not?" her sister demanded.

"Because Mom and Dad are going to Emerald Isle for the Goodens anniversary party, which means I don't have a babysitter."

"Isn't there someone else you usually call if Mom's busy?" Jordyn asked.

"Yeah," she admitted. "You."

"Well, that won't work," Jordyn said glumly. Then she brightened. "What about Ryder?"

Lauryn shook her head. "I'm not going to ask Ryder."

"Why not? Kylie and Zachary love him."

"Because Saturday is one of his rare days off and I'm not going to ask him to give it up to babysit my kids."

"Then I'll ask him," Jordyn said.

"Ask who what?" Ryder asked, coming over to join their conversation.

"No, you won't," Lauryn said pointedly.

Jordyn sighed but kept her lips zipped.

Ryder's glance shifted from one to the other questioningly until Lauryn finally explained. "Tristyn scheduled a spa day for Saturday, but my parents are going to be out of town."

"If you need someone to look after Kylie and Zachary, I'd be happy to," he said.

Jordyn shot her a triumphant look.

"I'll be gone most of the afternoon," she told him.

"And we might want to go for dinner after the spa," Jordyn added.

"That's not a problem. But if you end up at Marg & Rita's—" he winked at Lauryn "—I'd suggest taking it easy on the tequila."

Chapter Fifteen

After the big reveal episode had finished taping, Ryder helped Lauryn move her dishes and cookware back into the kitchen. Of course, the unpacking took twice as long as the packing because Kylie was running around the kitchen with her arms outstretched, pretending to be an airplane circling the island. Of course, Zachary thought his sister's antics were the funniest thing ever, and as he watched her through the mesh screen of his playpen, his whole body shook with his giggles.

"I love to listen to his laugh," Lauryn said to Ryder. "And to know, after wondering and worrying for so long, that they're both settled and happy now."

He slid an arm across her shoulders and drew her close to his side. "It doesn't look like you have anything to worry about now."

"Today has been a very good day," she agreed. "Thanks to you and your crew."

"While your words are appreciated, the guys are going to expect cookies when they come back on Monday," he told her.

"Then I guess I'll have to bake some cookies this weekend."

And she did. She found her favorite sugar cookie recipe and she spent Friday afternoon measuring and mixing and rolling and cutting. Of course, Kylie wanted to help, too, so she gave her daughter a portion of the dough and let her do her own thing. By the time Ryder showed up with pizza for dinner, she had six-dozen cookies in the shapes of hammers, saws and tape measures cooling on racks—and flour on every horizontal surface.

After they ate, they cleaned up the kitchen together. It didn't seem to matter to Ryder that she and Kylie had made the mess—he never hesitated to pitch in and help. Which gave her an idea...

"I was thinking about something we might do tonight, after the kids are in bed," she told him, as she was loading their dinner plates into her sparkling new dishwasher.

He finished wiping down the island, then folded the cloth over the faucet. "What's that?"

"It's something you suggested a while back but that I've resisted until now," she said.

"You have my complete and undivided attention," he assured her.

"It could get messy and sweaty," she warned, her tone deliberately provocative.

"Tell me more," he urged.

She laughed softly. "You don't have any idea what I'm suggesting, do you?"

"No," he admitted. "But I'm keeping an open mind."

"I'm talking about stripping—"

"Yes," he said, the word a heartfelt plea. "Please."

"—wallpaper."

"Oh."

She folded her arms over her chest. "That's a disappointing response considering how many times you've mentioned that you hate the plaid in the bedroom."

"Have I said a single word about it recently?" he asked.

"No," she admitted.

"Because when I'm with you, I don't see the wallpaper," he told her. "I don't see anything but you."

Her heart did a slow roll inside her chest. "You're good at that."

He put his arms around her. "At what?"

"Saying just the right thing so that I completely forget what we were talking about and just want to jump your bones."

He grinned. "Go ahead and jump—I'll catch you."

Ryder was happy to spend the day with Kylie and Zachary on Saturday, but he missed Lauryn. Somehow, in less than a week, he'd become accustomed to spending most of his free time with her. Regardless of whether they were hanging out with the kids or cuddling on the sofa together to watch television or snuggling naked in her bed, he was happy just to be with her.

He'd never before experienced the simple comfort of being with a woman without any particular plan or agenda—he'd never thought he wanted it. Until Lauryn. And although he was missing her, she deserved this time with her sisters, and he was glad—for a lot of reasons—that she'd taken it today.

When the kids were finally settled into their beds later that night, he had a whole new appreciation for what she did every day. Being a single parent was definitely not a job for the fainthearted.

He was picking up Barbie clothes and Candy Land pieces when he heard her key in the lock.

"Hey, you," he said, meeting Lauryn at the door.

"Hi," she responded in a whisper that matched his. "Where are the kids?"

"Sleeping."

She glanced at the watch on her wrist. "I didn't realize it had gotten so late."

"It's not all that late—just past their bedtime."

"Did they settle down without any trouble?" she asked.

"Without any trouble," he confirmed. "Although I have to confess—I wavered on the one-bedtime-story rule."

"How many did you read?"

"Three," he admitted.

Lauryn shook her head, but she was smiling. "Pushover."

He didn't deny it. "Did you have a good day?"

"I did," she confirmed. "Maybe the most surprising part is that I didn't worry about Kylie and Zachary at all. I thought about them, of course, and about you. But the whole time I was gone, I didn't worry because I knew you were taking care of them."

"I'm glad," he said sincerely.

"So what did you do with your day?"

"We went to the park, played twenty-three games of Candy Land, watched some princess movie and made peanut butter cookies."

"*You* made cookies with the kids?"

"With Kylie," he said. "Zachary was napping."

"What did you have for dinner?"

"Peanut butter cookies."

She looked so appalled he couldn't help but chuckle. "I'm kidding. We had chicken fingers and French fries with carrot and celery sticks, then peanut butter cookies for dessert. There are some left in the kitchen, if you want to try them."

"Maybe later," she said, sliding her palms up his chest. "Right now, I want to take you upstairs to my bed."

Her touch had an immediate and predictable effect on his body, but he tried to focus on their conversation while he still had some blood in his head. "And right now I really want to be taken upstairs," he agreed. "But there's something I need to tell you first."

She brushed her lips against his. "I'm listening."

"You had an unexpected visitor today."

"I'm not interested in anyone but you right now," she promised, starting to unfasten the buttons on his shirt.

He really didn't want to distract her from what she was

doing, but he knew she needed to hear this. "Not even your ex-husband?"

"What?" Lauryn dropped her hands and took a step back, her playful mood gone. "Why would you bring him up now?"

"Because he was here," Ryder said.

She shook her head, refusing to believe it. "He's in California."

"No, he's not," he said. "He showed up at your front door today, around three o'clock, grumbling about his key not working and demanding to know where you were."

"Are you sure it was Rob?" she asked, clearly hoping that he'd made a mistake.

"How many other men are there who would claim to be your husband?"

"*Ex*-husband," she said, firmly emphasizing the "ex."

But he could tell the news was finally starting to sink in, because she moved into the living room and lowered herself onto the arm of the sofa.

She looked up at him, the earlier sparkle in her eyes replaced by wariness. "He was really here?"

He nodded.

"But…why?"

"I don't know," he told her. "He didn't share his reasons with me."

She folded her arms over her chest, an instinctive and protective gesture. "Did Kylie see him?"

He shook his head. "No. She was in the kitchen, up to her elbows in peanut butter cookie dough, and I didn't let him past the front door."

She breathed out a weary sigh. "Thank you for that. I don't know what it would do to Kylie to see her father now, just when she's finally gotten used to him being gone."

He was more concerned about what it would do to Lauryn to see her ex-husband again. Yes, they were divorced, but he suspected that a piece of paper hadn't magically erased the feelings she'd had for the man she'd married—and the father of her children. And while he wasn't generally insecure, he couldn't deny that their shared history made him a little uneasy.

"If he's come back to see them, I don't know that you're going to be able to keep him away," Ryder warned gently.

"He left without even saying goodbye to Kylie," she reminded him. "He left before Zachary was even born."

"He's still their father."

She nodded, unable to deny that basic truth. "Was he a jerk to you?"

"Not really," he said. "He referred to me as the babysitter, but I don't think he meant to be deliberately insulting."

"I'm sorry," she said.

"Why are *you* apologizing?"

"Because I don't know what else to say—what to think," she admitted. "When he signed the separation agreement, I assumed that was it, that we were done forever and I wouldn't ever have to see him again. I certainly never expected that he would just show up at the door, and when I asked you to stay with the kids today, I didn't anticipate that you'd have to deal with him."

"Maybe you should call your cousin, the lawyer," Ryder suggested.

"I had a local attorney, Shelly Watts, handle the divorce for me," she told him. "Not that there was much to handle, but she drafted the terms of our separation agreement, he signed it, and the judge granted the divorce."

"Then you should call her."

"Now?"

He glanced at the clock. "Probably not now. Assuming your attorney has a life outside of the law, she might not want to be interrupted at nine thirty on a Saturday night. But definitely in the morning—to let her know what's going on."

"How can I tell her what's going on when I don't have a clue? For all I know, he came back for the leather jacket he left in the back of his closet."

"Maybe," he acknowledged. "But he introduced himself as your husband, not your ex-husband."

"So?"

"So…" He hesitated, reluctant to even speak the thought aloud. But he knew that, as unpalatable as it was to him, she needed to consider the possibility—and so did he. "Maybe he came back because he wants *you* back."

She pushed herself up from the sofa and headed toward the stairs. Ryder followed her up to the landing, watching from the doorway of Kylie's room as she tiptoed across the floor to check on her daughter, pulling up her covers and bending to touch her lips to the little girl's cheek. Then she crossed the hall to Zachary's room and followed the same routine with him.

"I called Rob after Zachary was born," she told Ryder now, her voice barely more than a whisper. "No one knows about that—not even my sisters."

"I don't think they'd be surprised to hear that you reached out to your husband to let him know that you'd given birth to his child."

"Maybe not," she acknowledged. "But it was more than that. I asked him to come home—no, I practically *begged* him to come home, to give us another chance to be a family."

He looked at the beautiful, strong, stubborn woman in front of him and his heart sank as he realized there could only be one reason she would do something like that. "You were still in love with him."

And if she was then, maybe she was now.

But Lauryn shook her head. "I didn't still love him. I didn't even *like* him very much at that point. But I looked at my baby and I felt that I owed it to him to try to give him a real family."

"Do you think that's why he's back?" And if it was, would she be willing to give her ex-husband that second chance now?

She shook her head again. "Rob's never cared about anyone but Rob, and I don't care where he goes or what he does," she insisted, though the tears that shone in her eyes suggested otherwise. "But this is so unfair to the children. Zachary is such a happy baby, and Kylie hasn't had a panic attack in weeks. And now...just seeing him could turn her whole world upside down again."

"What about your world?" Ryder asked.

"My children are my world," she reminded him.

"And me?" he wondered. "What am I?"

She was quiet for a minute, as if considering her response. "You're my 'one day at a time,'" she finally said, referring back to the conversation they'd had the first night they were together.

And that was all he'd wanted to be then—or so he'd believed. But now... "What if I want to be more than that?"

She closed her eyes. "Please don't do this. Not now."

He wanted to press her for an answer, but she was right. This wasn't the time. She needed to focus on her children and what her ex-husband's return would mean to them. They would have plenty of time to figure out their own relationship later—he hoped.

"Okay," he relented. "Tell me what you want me to do."

She looked up at him, those beautiful gray-green eyes filled with desperation. "I want you to take me to bed and let me pretend that we never had this conversation," she said, lifting her sweater over her head and tossing it aside, revealing a silky purple demi-cup bra and lots of tantalizing skin. "Help me forget about everything but the way I feel when I'm with you."

It wasn't much, but if it was the only thing he could do for her, he would give it his very best effort.

Lauryn didn't know what time Ryder left, she only knew that when she woke up in the early hours of the morning, he was gone. Her bed always seemed so much bigger and emptier without him, but this morning—with the specter of her ex-husband's return in the forefront of her mind— she felt even more alone.

She'd lain awake for half the night wondering why Rob had come back to Charisma, to no avail. What she did know was that if he was determined to see her, he wouldn't wait too long to show up at her door again.

As soon as she was up and dressed, she called Jordyn and asked her if she could take the kids for a few hours. He was waiting on the front porch—sitting in her favorite chair with his feet propped up on the railing—when she returned.

She tucked her keys in her pocket, because she had no intention of unlocking the door and inviting him inside. "So the rumors are true," she said.

"You heard I was back," he guessed.

"Why are you here, Rob?"

"California was too far away from my wife and kids," he said, his tone as deliberately casual as his pose.

"*Ex*-wife," she said pointedly.

"You asked me to come back," he reminded her. "To give us another chance to be a family."

"That was eight months ago. I'd just given birth and still had a lot of drugs in my system," she said by way of explanation.

"Don't tell me it's too late," he said, the plea accompanied by his most charming smile.

That smile used to make her forgive him all manner of things, but it had no power over her anymore. "It's way past too late, so why don't you tell me what you really want?"

"I'm hurt that you don't trust I'm telling you the truth," he said, his tone as false as the claim.

"I learned the hard way not to trust anything that comes out of your mouth," she said bluntly.

He dropped his feet from the railing and stood up, moving closer to her. She had to tip her head back to meet his gaze, but she held her ground.

"We were married for five and a half years," he said, lowering his voice to a more intimate tone. "I don't believe that your feelings for me are gone."

"Our five-and-a-half-year marriage ended when you ran off with the twenty-two-year-old you were screwing in your office at The Locker Room."

He finally took a step back. "Speaking of The Locker Room," he said, pointedly ignoring the rest of her statement, "I went by the store and saw that you changed the name."

"I've made a lot of changes there, and in the rest of my life," she told him.

He nodded as he looked around. "New porch, new roof, new lover."

She narrowed her gaze on him. "Is there a point to this or are you just talking out loud?"

"I was hoping you would deny that you're sleeping with your babysitter."

"It's none of your business who I'm sleeping with," she said, pleased that her cool tone gave no hint of the fury churning inside.

"I just never expected that you'd do something so… tawdry."

She shrugged. "I couldn't find a hunky yoga instructor. And he's not the babysitter—he's Ryder Wallace."

He seemed surprised by this revelation. "The host of that home renovation show?"

"Yes," she admitted.

He shrugged. "Well, he's not your usual type, but I guess

you saw the benefits of having a man around who didn't mind banging up some drywall after he finished banging you."

She curled her fingers around the porch railing and managed to resist the urge to slap his smirking face. "You are every bit the ass that Tristyn always thought you were."

"You think I don't know that your family never approved of me? That no one ever thought I was good enough for you?" he asked bitterly. "They all stood around watching me, waiting for me to fail."

She shook her head. "I'm not going to claim that everyone was overjoyed when we told them we were getting married, but they would have done anything to support us because you were my husband. You were the only one who felt the need to compete with my family."

Rob slid his foot along one of the new boards in the porch. "Did Daddy write a check for all of the work you've had done around here? Or did you have money hidden away that you failed to disclose when we settled our finances?"

"There were no assets—only debts," she snapped back at him. "And most of those were your debts."

"For richer or poorer," he reminded her.

"So it was just the faithful part of the vows that you couldn't remember?" she challenged.

"Let's not throw stones," he admonished.

"I'd rather throw you off my property, anyway," she shot back.

"We bought this house together," he reminded her.

"With money from my parents."

"Money they gave to us in celebration of our marriage."

She shook her head. "Have you rewritten our entire history in your mind?"

"We had a lot of good times together," he said.

"The good times were a long time ago," she told him. "And memory lane is closed."

His tone grew cold. "I'm entitled to see my kids."

Which was what she'd both anticipated and feared. And while she wanted to refuse, she knew that she couldn't. It didn't matter that he'd been a horrible husband or a neglectful parent—he was still the father of her children. And when she'd talked to her attorney earlier that morning, Shelly had warned her that Kylie's abandonment issues were as inconsequential as the fact that Zachary didn't even know his father. Absent evidence of abuse, no judge would deny Rob access to his children.

"They're not here right now," she said, grateful that it was true.

"You can't stop me from seeing them," he warned her.

"I don't want to stop you from seeing them," she said, although that wasn't exactly true. "I just want to know the truth about why you're here and how long you're planning to stay before you turn their lives upside down."

"I'm here because I missed my family," he insisted.

"The daughter you barely spent any time with and the son you've never even seen because you took off before he was born?" she challenged.

He dropped his gaze. "I panicked," he told her. "I knew the business was in trouble. I was barely bringing home enough money to pay the bills and put food on the table, and soon we were going to have another baby and another mouth to feed. I just couldn't bear to fail you."

"And screwing the yoga instructor somehow fixed all of that?" she asked derisively.

"I made mistakes," he admitted. "But I have the right to be with my kids."

"I'm not going to oppose visitation," she told him. She would fight tooth and nail if he tried to go after custody, but she was going to try to play nice—for now. "If you really want to see your children, meet us at Oakridge Park at two o'clock."

Chapter Sixteen

When Lauryn headed to the park with the kids, she didn't tell Kylie that her daddy would be there. She'd learned a long time ago not to count on her ex-husband for anything, and she didn't want her daughter to experience the same disappointment of being let down by a man she should be able to count on.

After all, the first man any little girl falls in love with is her father, and she knew that Rob's abandonment of his daughter had left deep scars. Thankfully, Kylie's life was filled with men she could depend on: her grandfather, her uncles and now Ryder.

But she couldn't think about Ryder now. She couldn't let herself be distracted.

It was a short walk to the park but the wind was brisk, and Lauryn was glad she'd put a hat and mittens on Kylie and tucked a blanket around Zachary.

"Can I go on the swings, Mama?" Kylie asked, as soon as the playground was within her sight.

"Of course," Lauryn agreed. "But I think there's someone over by the slide who wants to see you."

Kylie immediately pivoted in that direction, a bright smile lighting her whole face. "Wyder?"

"No, honey—it's Daddy."

"Daddy?" Kylie echoed, sounding more confused than excited. "Daddy's in Califownia."

"He came from California for a visit," she explained, hoping he wouldn't stay much longer than that.

Kylie, so eager to skip ahead a moment ago, stuck close to her mother now.

Lauryn couldn't blame her daughter for being wary, and she hated that she'd felt compelled to make this visit happen. Just because Rob was here today wasn't any guarantee that he would be around tomorrow. In fact, she hoped he wouldn't be around tomorrow, but she was following her attorney's advice and cooperating—at least for now.

She bent down to unhook Zachary's belt, then lifted the baby from his stroller. He looked so much like her own father—actually both of her children favored the Garrett side—but the deep blue eyes that he shared with his sister were undoubtedly inherited from their dad. Would Rob recognize that fact? Would he feel anything when he looked at his son for the first time?

He crouched down in front of his daughter. "Hello, Kylie."

She smiled a little shyly. "Hi, Daddy."

"You've grown about six inches since I last saw you," he told her.

"I'm in pweschool now."

"Preschool already?" he said, sounding impressed.

"I'm fwee," she said, holding up three fingers.

He nodded. "I know. You had a birthday in April."

"Wif balloons an' choc'ate cupcakes."

"I'm sorry I missed it," he told her.

"You missed Zach's birfday, too. When he was borned."

He nodded again. "I've missed a lot."

"You were in Califownia," she said, as if that was a perfectly reasonable explanation for everything. Then she turned to Lauryn. "Can I go on the swings now, Mama?"

"Go ahead."

"You come push?" Kylie asked her.

"I'll be there in a minute," she promised.

"I wasn't kidding about how big she is," Rob remarked.

"You've been gone almost a year," she reminded him. "And kids grow up fast."

His gaze shifted to the baby. "Kylie was so little when she was born."

"And Zachary was just a little bigger than her, but he was sixteen pounds at his last checkup."

"Can I...hold him?"

"Of course," she agreed. He'd been so hesitant with Kylie when she was a baby, but at almost nine months, Zachary was solid and sturdy.

Rob took the baby from her. He didn't look entirely comfortable holding his son, but she couldn't deny that he was making an effort.

"He has your eyes," Lauryn pointed out to him.

"Do you think so?" Rob sounded pleased by this revelation and took a closer look at the baby now. "And your ears and your dad's chin."

She nodded.

"We might have made some mistakes in our marriage," he noted, "but we made beautiful babies together."

"And you took their education savings along with all of the money from our joint accounts," she reminded him. "What did you do with it?"

He couldn't meet her gaze as he admitted, "I invested in Roxi's yoga studio."

"And ran that business into the ground, too?" she guessed.

"Actually, she's doing very well in California," he told her. "Of course, it helps that more than one Hollywood A-lister has been seen entering and exiting 'Yoga Rox.'"

"Yoga Rocks?" she echoed dubiously.

"Rox with an *x*—like Roxi," he said.

And she'd worried that the Sports Destination's slogan was cheesy. "But if everything is going so well in California, why are you here?"

He sighed. "I didn't know where else to go."

"She kicked you out, didn't she?"

"We decided that we wanted different things," he hedged.

"What different things?"

"For starters, she wanted a baby," he admitted. "And I decided that if I was going to be a father, it should be to the kids I already had."

"How very noble," she said dryly.

He shrugged. "And maybe I panicked a little."

Again.

"Do you love her?" Lauryn asked him.

"I think I do," he confided. "But I loved you, too, and I still screwed up. How do I know I won't do the same with Roxi?"

"You don't," she said. "Love isn't perfect and relationships don't come with guarantees. You just have to be willing to open your heart and follow where it leads." An important lesson that she was only starting to learn herself and only because of Ryder's presence in her life.

"Mama!" Kylie called, clearly growing impatient with waiting.

So Lauryn turned toward the swings, and her ex-husband, with their baby in his arms, walked beside her.

The first visit between Rob and the kids went well enough that her ex-husband asked if he could see them again the next day. While Lauryn intended to accommodate reasonable visitation, she didn't think two days in a row was either reasonable or in the best interests of her children, especially Kylie, who was as confused by her father's reappearance in her life as she'd been by his disappearance eleven months earlier. But she did agree to the day after that, and then two days after that again.

Ryder found Lauryn in her office, doing something on the computer, when he stopped by the store a few days later.

"You look busy," he noted.

She glanced up and smiled, and he felt the now-familiar

tug at his heart that warned he was well and truly hooked. The bigger surprise was that he didn't mind at all.

"Not too busy for you," she promised. "What's up?"

"I had to make a trip to the hardware store to pick up grout for the bathroom and I thought I'd stop by to say hi."

She clicked the mouse to save the updates, then pushed her chair away from the desk and crossed the room to kiss him. "Hi."

He slid his arms around her and kissed her again, longer and deeper. "Hello."

"Do you have time for lunch?" she asked him.

"Unfortunately not," he said, sincerely regretful. "But we've been invited to dinner at Avery and Justin's tonight."

"Oh, um, tonight?"

"Is there a problem with tonight?" he asked, surprised by her reluctance.

She nodded slowly. "I'm sorry, but I told Rob that he could take the kids out for pizza tonight."

"He's not taking them on his own," Ryder guessed.

"Of course not."

"So you made plans to go out with your ex-husband and didn't tell me?" he noted.

"Because it has nothing to do with you."

The matter-of-fact tone sliced into him as effectively as the words. And though he didn't respond, the flexing of the muscle in his jaw must have given away his feelings.

"And now you're mad," she realized.

"Why would I be mad? I'm just the guy you're currently sleeping with—why would I care that you're having dinner with your ex-husband? *It has nothing to do with me.*"

She winced as he tossed the words back at her. "I didn't mean it like that."

"I think you did mean it exactly like that." And that truth was like a sucker punch to his gut. He turned toward the door.

Lauryn grabbed his arm, attempting to halt his retreat. "Ryder, please don't do this. Don't walk away mad."

"Mad is the least of what I'm feeling right now," he told her, his tone quiet and remarkably controlled despite the emotions churning inside him.

Her eyes filled with tears. "I'm sorry."

He just shook his head.

"None of this has been easy for me," she told him. "I'm trying to do what's best for my children. And as much as I wish Rob had never come back to Charisma, I can't pretend that he's not here. And I can't deny Kylie and Zachary the chance to know their father."

"It takes a lot more than biology to be a father," he said bluntly. "And a man who walked out on them once already doesn't deserve the title."

"Maybe not," she acknowledged. "But he's the only one they've got."

"If you really believe that—" He shook his head, unable to speak aloud the words that would completely destroy what he'd thought they were building together.

Instead, he walked away.

His mood didn't change at all throughout the rest of the day, so he went home in a pissy mood and woke up Saturday morning the same way. But he was okay with that—he knew his anger and frustration were justified. What bothered him more, what churned inside his gut, was the hurt she'd so easily caused with a few casual and careless words.

His anger was manageable—he could pick up a sledge-hammer and pound something until he'd taken the edge off. The hurt made him feel like a teenage girl dumped on prom night. And the two emotions tangled up together ensured that he was less than welcoming when he responded to the knock at his door.

"What are you doing here?" he asked his sister.

Avery held up the plate she carried. "Leftover coconut cream pie from the dinner you didn't show up for last night—I've eaten too much of it already and wanted to get it out of the house."

Ryder stood back to allow her to enter, then he opened the kitchen drawer for a fork, peeled back the plastic wrap and dug into the pie.

"I didn't expect you to eat it now," she said.

"I'm hungry now," he told her.

"And grumpy," she deduced. "Do you want to tell me what caused this particular mood you're in?"

"Nope."

"Then I'll guess," she warned.

"Don't."

Avery sighed. "Does it have anything to do with Lauryn's ex-husband being back in town?"

He scowled. "How do you know about that?"

"My husband's a Garrett, too," she reminded him. "And I'm sorry if it seems like I'm butting in, but I don't want you to get hurt."

While he appreciated the sentiment, it was already too late.

"She's got a lot of baggage," she said gently.

"Don't we all?"

"Not in the form of an ex-husband and two kids," she pointed out. "And now that their father is back..."

"What?"

His sister sighed. "You need to understand that it's natural for most mothers to put the needs of their children ahead of their own."

"You think I don't understand that?"

"I don't think you're prepared for the possibility that Lauryn might decide to give her ex-husband a second chance, to give her children back their father, and I'm afraid it will break your heart if she does."

He couldn't deny that it would—or that his heart was already battered and bruised. And as uncomfortable as the feeling was, it was also a revelation.

"Did you know," he said to his sister now, "that for a long time, I thought my legacy from our dear mom was to be as closed off and detached as she is?"

She looked at him, stunned. "Why would you ever believe such a thing?"

Ryder just shrugged. "How many guys get to be my age without having had their hearts broken at least once?"

"So why Lauryn?" she asked.

"I don't know," he admitted. "There was just something there from the first time I set eyes on her. And I know this is going to sound corny as hell, but it's like my heart was locked up and she was the only one who had the key."

His sister's eyes misted. "Damn, you really do love her, don't you?"

"I really do," he said.

"Have you told her?" she asked.

He shook his head.

"Don't you think you should?"

"Not right now," he decided. "Not when everything is so up in the air with her ex-husband."

"But that's exactly when—and why—she needs to know how you feel," Avery told him. "If he is making a play for Lauryn, she's going to be forced to make a choice—the father of her children who claims he made a mistake and still loves her? Or the fun-loving guy who's promised her nothing more than a good time?"

He scowled at that. "She knows how much I care about her."

Avery gave him a pointed look. "You better hope she does."

Chapter Seventeen

A few days after Ryder walked out of her office, on another day that Rob was scheduled to visit with Kylie and Zachary, a rainstorm eliminated the possibility of a meeting at the park. Lauryn didn't want to invite her ex-husband into her home because she was finally starting to feel as if it was *hers*, but she knew he didn't have any other place to take them.

She'd asked him about job prospects, because she was curious to know if he was serious about staying in Charisma or just putting in time until he figured things out. He told her, not very convincingly, that he'd been looking, then had the nerve to suggest that she could hire him to work at Sports Destination. She turned him down, clearly and unequivocally, and mentally crossed her fingers that he'd decide his options were better in California.

With other parts of the house under construction, she asked him to try to confine the kids to the living room, and then she left to run some errands. When she returned from her grocery shopping, she was relieved that he'd managed to do so, because the room was a disaster but at least it was the only room that was a disaster.

Kylie was on the floor, putting together a puzzle, and Zachary was slowly cruising around the table—a very recent development, gaining more strength and confidence with every step.

"Did everything go okay?" she asked cautiously.

"Zach peed on Daddy," Kylie informed her eagerly.

Rob shrugged, looking sheepish. "I've never changed a baby boy's diaper before."

And not many baby girl diapers, either, but she didn't bother to remind him of that fact.

"Other than that, I think it went well," he told her. "We had a good time, didn't we, Kylie?"

The little girl nodded.

"I'm glad," Lauryn said.

"Do you mean that?"

"Of course, I do. If you really want a relationship with Kylie and Zachary, I won't stand in the way."

"What if I really want a relationship with you?"

She glanced at her daughter, who appeared to be engrossed in what she was doing but was undoubtedly absorbing every word of their conversation.

"Kylie, I got some of those fruit cups you like, if you want a snack before dinner."

Of course, her always-hungry daughter eagerly abandoned her puzzle.

"Please make sure you sit at the table so you don't spill it."

"I will," Kylie promised.

"What was that about?" Rob asked.

"That was about not wanting our daughter to get any ideas about a reconciliation, because it's not going to happen. I've moved on with my life and so have you. You're just looking for the comfort of something familiar because you're feeling lost and lonely right now."

"You fell in love with me once," he reminded her. "If you give me a chance, I'm confident you'll fall in love with me again."

She shook her head. "Have you listened to a single word I've said?"

"Of course, I have. But I'm asking you to think about our children—"

"Don't you dare tell me to think about our children," she

said, her voice low but sharp. "Every single day, everything I do, I do for them."

"So tell me what I can do," he said, duly chastised.

"You're supposed to be figuring out what you really want," she reminded him. "And not using Kylie and Zachary—or me—to fill the emptiness in your life."

"I know what I want," he said.

Then he pressed his mouth to hers.

Lauryn shoved him away with both hands, shocked by his audacity. "What the—"

"Excuse me for interrupting," Ryder said coolly from the doorway.

At the sound of his voice, Zachary's attention shifted immediately from the stuffed dog he'd found to the man in the doorway. With the toy still clutched in his fist, he dropped to the ground and began crawling toward him.

"You're not interrupting," Lauryn said, mentally crossing her fingers that he hadn't witnessed her ex-husband's impulsive kiss. Since she'd declined the invitation to have dinner with his sister, Ryder had been giving her space. A lot more space than she wanted. And while she didn't know how to bridge the gap between him, she was pretty sure that kissing her ex-husband would not help her cause.

"I need your approval of the hardware for the master bathroom before the guys start to install it," he told her.

She was surprised by the request. "Didn't I already sign off on it?"

He shook his head as he glanced down at the baby, who had reached his destination and was now pulling himself up to a standing position by holding on to the leg of Ryder's pants. "What are you doing, big guy?"

Zachary responded with a droolly smile.

"No." Ryder kept his focus on the baby as he responded to her question. "The manufacturer couldn't supply your first choice—this is the alternate."

"Okay. I'll come take a look."

"We were in the middle of something here," Rob reminded her.

"No," she said bluntly. "We weren't."

Kylie, her snack apparently finished, came back to the room to finish her puzzle. When she saw Zachary with her favorite stuffed dog in his hand, she snatched the toy from him.

"Mine," she told him.

Of course, the abrupt loss of the toy caused her brother to burst into tears.

Ryder started to reach for the baby, instinctively wanting to soothe his distress. Then he glanced in Rob's direction and apparently thought better of it.

"Kylie," Lauryn admonished wearily, lifting Zachary into her arms.

"But it's mine," Kylie said, her own eyes filling with tears as she hugged the toy to her chest. "He always takes what's mine."

"Come here, baby," Rob said, holding out his arms to his daughter.

But Kylie turned away from him and threw herself at Ryder, wrapping her arms around his legs and sobbing dramatically, which did not please her father.

Ryder lowered his head to whisper something to Kylie, who drew in a deep, shuddery breath and relinquished her viselike grip on him.

"I'll be there in just a minute," Lauryn told him.

He nodded and turned to head back up the stairs.

"Well, that was...enlightening," Rob said.

Lauryn wasn't quite sure how to respond. While she would have preferred if her ex-husband had stayed gone, he had been making an effort to get to know his children, and it had to hurt to see how attached they were to the other man.

"They've seen Ryder almost every day for the past six weeks," she told him.

"Are you really trying to make me feel better?" Rob mocked her effort. "Isn't it my own fault that my kids don't know me?"

"It's a simple fact," she said. "Fault doesn't matter."

"I guess it's like the song says—you don't know what you've got until it's gone. And it is gone, isn't it?"

She nodded.

And when he was finally gone, too, she called Tristyn again. "I need a favor."

Ryder didn't stick around to see how long Lauryn's ex-husband stayed. He took a list of supplies that were required and headed to the hardware store.

He'd been right about the ex. The guy had come back to make another play for the woman he'd been foolish enough to walk away from, and while Ryder had been tempted to punch him in the face when he saw his hands on Lauryn, he'd held himself back. After all, it had nothing to do with him.

But several hours later, when he was staring at but not really watching the football game on television, she showed up at his door.

"Do you remember when I said that Kylie and Zachary were my world and you wanted to know what you were to me?" she asked him.

He tucked his hands in his pockets to prevent himself from reaching for her. "I remember that you didn't really answer the question."

"Well, I'm ready to answer it now."

"Okay," he said cautiously.

"You are my gravity," she said.

He wasn't quite sure how to interpret that. "I weigh you down?"

She shook her head, the corners of her mouth lifting just a little. "You keep me grounded. And—" she lifted her arms to link them behind his neck "—you are the force that attracts my body."

"Am I?" His hands came out of his pockets and went around her, so that she was in his embrace.

"Yes." She drew his mouth down to hers. "For the past four days, I feel as if I've been floating without any direction or purpose." She brushed her lips against his. "I've missed you, Ryder."

He kissed her back, savoring the sweet softness of her mouth. He'd missed her, too. He'd missed this. "You're making it hard for me to stay mad at you," he admitted.

"Good, because I don't want you to be mad at me." She pressed closer to him. "I'm sorry I hurt you. To be honest, I didn't know that I could. I didn't know what any of this meant to you."

"Then let me make it clear—I love you, Lauryn." He sucked in a breath and blew it out again, a little unsteadily. "And that's the first time I've ever said those words to a woman who isn't related to me," he confided, "so let me try it again. I love you, Lauryn." This time he smiled afterward. "And I love Kylie and Zachary, too. I understand that you have to figure out what's best for them, but I want to be a factor in that equation, too."

She hugged him tight. "You are an essential factor in that equation." And began to unfasten his shirt. "Let me show you how essential."

"You don't fight fair," he protested.

"I don't want to fight at all." Parting the fabric, she pressed her lips to his skin, where his heart was beating for her.

He didn't want to fight, either. Not when the alternative was so tantalizing. But he held her at arm's length long enough to ask, "Who's with the kids now?"

"Tristyn."

He lifted her sweater over her head, tossed it aside. "What time is she expecting you home?"

"I warned her I might be late."

"You're going to be very late," he confirmed.

Then he lifted her into his arms and carried her to his bed.

He'd told her he loved her.

Several days later, Lauryn was still marveling over that fact—and wondering if he'd noticed that she'd never said the words back. Not because she didn't feel the same way, but because she was determined to take their relationship one day at a time. With her ex-husband still in town, his presence an almost-daily reminder of that failed relationship, it seemed wise.

She was putting more hours in at the store again as the community embraced Sports Destination and business continued to pick up. Adam wanted to hire another part-time employee in anticipation of the holiday rush, and she was giddy anticipating that there might actually *be* a holiday rush. In fact, she was so caught up in preparations for the post-Thanksgiving sales she nearly forgot about Thanksgiving itself and might have done so if Ryder hadn't asked about her plans.

"My mom and my aunts play hostess on a rotating schedule for major holidays," she told him. "I think we're at my Aunt Jane's house this time."

"Thanksgiving is in five days and you *think* it's at your Aunt Jane's?"

She opened the calendar app on her phone and scrolled to the date, then nodded. "Aunt Jane's at four o'clock."

"Were you planning to invite me to go with you?" he asked.

"I didn't think you'd be interested in that kind of thing," she admitted. "And it's usually pretty chaotic. With all of my aunts, uncles and cousins, there will probably be thirty people there."

"I like people," he assured her. "And I really like turkey."

"Then I guess there's no reason you can't come with us," she decided.

"So why does it sound as if you're looking for a reason?"

"I'm not," she said. "I'm just wondering what to tell people... How to explain our...situation."

"Our situation?" he echoed, amused. "I believe it's called a relationship. And one of the basic rules of a relationship is that the people involved usually make an effort to be together on national holidays and other special occasions."

"That's a rule?" she asked.

He nodded solemnly. "One of the big ones."

"All right. Would you like to spend Thanksgiving with me and the kids and the rest of my family?"

"I'd love to," he told her.

"Okay," she agreed. "But if you get the third degree from my dad and my uncles and half of my cousins, don't say I didn't warn you."

Two days before Thanksgiving, Lauryn was in her office with Adam, reviewing purchase orders for the summer retail season, when there was a knock on the open door.

"Hey, Lauryn. Do you have a minute?" Rob asked.

She looked questioningly at her manager.

"I'll go help Bree unpack the shipment that came in yesterday afternoon," he offered.

"Thank you." She turned her attention to her ex-husband, waiting for him to tell her why he'd stopped by—because she knew there had to be a reason.

"I talked to Roxi this morning," he finally said. "She's pregnant."

Lauryn took a minute to digest the information. "Yours?"

He nodded.

"Congratulations."

"Thanks."

"You don't sound very excited," she noted.

"I'm not sure how I'm supposed to feel," he admitted. "I know I haven't been a very good father to Kylie—or a father at all to Zachary."

"Maybe the third time's the charm," she suggested.

"Maybe," he said a little dubiously.

"How does this affect your plans here?" she asked. Because she really didn't care that he'd knocked up his girlfriend except insofar as it affected her children.

"She's willing to give me another chance," he told her. "And to put me in charge of the retail side of her business."

"So you're going back to California?"

He nodded, and she slowly released the breath she'd been holding.

"Are you going to marry her?"

"Roxi doesn't believe that a relationship needs to be sanctioned by religious or government authorities," he said, obviously quoting his girlfriend.

"The baby might change her mind about that," Lauryn told him.

"Maybe," he said again, with little enthusiasm. "You know, when we got married, I really thought we'd be together forever."

"So did I."

"I don't know when that changed," he admitted. "But somewhere along the line, I started to realize that I was letting you down. And that was the beginning of a vicious cycle—I felt like a terrible husband, so I acted like a terrible husband."

"I never had any grand ideals or expectations," she said. "I just wanted us to be partners in our marriage, to work together and build a family."

"And when I failed to do my part, you managed everything without me. You never needed me."

"That's not true," she denied.

"Maybe you wanted me," he allowed, "but you didn't

really need me. I failed you in so many ways, and you just did whatever needed to be done. You took care of the house, the baby, everything, and so competently I couldn't help but feel extraneous.

"Roxi isn't like you," he said now. "Being on her own for the past couple of weeks has made her realize that she needs me—and I think, maybe, I need to be needed."

"Your children need you." As much as she would like to see the back of him, she had to think about Kylie and Zachary and what was best for them. And she couldn't help but worry about the void his absence would again leave in the lives of their children—especially Kylie's.

"No, they don't. Not really. They're already more bonded to your new boyfriend than they are to me."

She couldn't deny that was true and she refused to feel guilty about it. If she felt guilty for anything, it was telling Ryder that her ex-husband was the only father her children had, because she knew now that wasn't true. Ryder had been there for both Kylie and Zachary in so many ways, proving that actions were a stronger measure than biology when it came to parenting.

"If I had any doubts about that, they were put to rest that day at your house—when Kylie and Zachary both turned to him instead of me. That's when I realized that I either needed to figure out how to be the full-time father my kids deserve or let them get on with their lives without me. But if I stay here, I'm abandoning another kid—Roxi's baby."

"Go back to California," she advised. "Take this second chance to be a dad—and do it right this time."

He seemed surprised—and grateful—that she was letting him off the hook, then he nodded. "I'm going to try." He stood up and hugged her. "Have a good life, Lauryn."

"I will," she said. "Good luck to you."

As Rob was on his way out, he passed Ryder on his way in. "How long were you standing there?" Lauryn asked.

"Long enough," he said. "But I had no intention of interrupting what looked like a goodbye."

"It *was* a goodbye," she assured him. "Rob's going back to the west coast."

"How do you feel about that?" he asked cautiously.

"A lot relieved and a little sad—not that he's leaving but that he couldn't be the father Kylie and Zachary deserve."

"Lucky for them, they've got a really awesome mom."

And you, she wanted to tell him. Because she'd finally recognized the truth he'd alluded to that day in her office. And although he seemed to have forgiven her thoughtlessly cruel words, Lauryn was determined to make it up to him by loving him for as long as he would let her.

Lauryn had always enjoyed celebrating the holidays with her extended family. She considered herself fortunate that she'd grown up with not just two sisters but a whole bunch of cousins, and as those cousins married and had babies, she was happy to see the next generation hanging out together.

She was even happier to see Braden sitting on the sofa in Aunt Jane's living room with Vanessa in his arms. It was no secret that her cousin loved kids—or that he and his wife had been trying for several years to have one of their own. During that time, they'd skipped a lot of family gatherings. Lauryn knew it had to be difficult for both of them to be surrounded by other people's babies, so she was thrilled to see that they were here today—and that Braden was playing the doting uncle.

Lauryn took her glass of wine and settled onto the sofa beside him. "She's gorgeous, isn't she?"

"Of course, she's a Garrett," Braden said immodestly. Then he glanced across the room to where Justin's wife was in conversation with his own. "Although her mom's got pretty good genes, too."

"Speaking of her mom—how did you manage to wrestle Vanessa away from Avery?"

"No wrestling required," he said. "I just told her that I needed practice for when our baby comes."

Lauryn's gaze immediately shifted from his smiling face to that of his not obviously pregnant wife across the room. "Are you… I mean, is Dana…"

He shook his head. "No, she's not pregnant. But if all goes according to plan, we'll have our own bundle of joy before the end of the year."

"What's the plan?" she asked cautiously.

"A private adoption. We've already signed the papers, we're just waiting for the baby to be born."

"Oh, Braden, that's wonderful," she said, sincerely thrilled for her cousin and his wife.

"It is," he agreed. "Although we're trying not to get too excited about it. Even though we've met with the birth mother and she's adamant that this is what she wants, there's always a possibility that she'll change her mind when she holds her baby in her arms."

Lauryn nodded, already praying that Braden and Dana wouldn't suffer such a heartbreaking disappointment. They'd both been through so much already.

"The way this family's been growing, we're going to need another table for holiday meals pretty soon," she said, focusing on the positive.

"Speaking of additions to the family," Braden said, grinning, "tell me about the new guy in your life."

While Lauryn was catching up with Braden in the family room, Ryder had been cornered by Jordyn in the den. Over the past couple of months, he'd gotten to know both of Lauryn's sisters pretty well—and he knew that none of them had any secrets from the others. And while Tristyn had given an enthusiastic thumbs-up to Lauryn's relationship with him, he sensed that Jordyn was still reserving judgment.

"You must be getting close to finishing up the renovations at Lauryn's house," she noted.

"It won't be too much longer," he confirmed.

"And then what happens?" she prompted.

"Are you inquiring about the schedule for my crew or asking about my personal plans?"

"I shouldn't be asking about anything," she admitted. "Lauryn would be the first to tell me that your relationship is none of my business, but she's had a rough year and I'm a little concerned that her feelings for you aren't reciprocated to the same degree."

"You're right—our relationship isn't any of your business," he agreed. "But I know you're motivated by concern, so I'll tell you—I'm in love with your sister."

The furrow between Jordyn's brows eased a little. "The ring-on-her-finger, forever-after kind of love?"

"Do you want to see the ring?" he asked. He'd bought a diamond solitaire a few days earlier, when he'd realized that he couldn't imagine his future without Lauryn in it. He still had a lot to learn about family, but he was confident that she could teach him everything he needed to know.

"You have a ring?" Jordyn asked, surprised excitement successfully pushing aside any lingering apprehension.

"I have a ring," he confirmed. "But I'd appreciate it if you kept that bit of information between us for now."

"I'll keep your secret," she said. "But don't wait too long to ask her—I'd like to be a bridesmaid before next summer."

He grinned. "I'll see what I can do."

Chapter Eighteen

The day after Thanksgiving, while most people were either sleeping off their overindulgence or racing for Black Friday sales, Ryder's crew was back on the job, eager to finish up so that they might enjoy an extended break over the Christmas holiday. And Lauryn was continuing to celebrate all the reasons she had to be thankful, because Kylie didn't seem bothered at all by the news that her father had gone back to California. Of course, Ryder's presence more than filled the void, and watching the sexy handyman with her children, Lauryn found herself starting to believe that maybe her real Prince Charming did wear a tool belt.

She was smiling at the thought as she carried a basket of clothes up to Kylie's room, the sounds of the men working almost like background music to her now. She'd thought she would hate the noise and debris and especially the intrusion into her home and her life, but over the past couple of months, she'd grown accustomed to the high-pitched buzz of saws and rhythmic *thunk* of nail guns that somehow blended together to create a not-unpleasant melody. In fact, she was beginning to suspect that she might miss the crew when they packed up and cleared out after the last stage of the renovation was complete.

Across the hall in the master bedroom, Stan and Brody were completing what Ryder referred to as punch-out work—the last-minute small details that needed to be taken care of before a job was done. She was eager to see the finished project—and excited to sleep in an actual bed again rather than the futon in the den that had been her temporary quarters while the renovations in her bedroom were underway.

She could hear the men talking, but she wasn't really listening until she heard them mention Watkinsville. The name snagged her attention because she remembered Ryder telling her that was the location of the antebellum mansion he was hoping to restore. She paused in the doorway of Kylie's room, hugging the laundry basket close to her chest as she shamelessly eavesdropped on their conversation.

"Are you planning to go?" Stan asked his coworker.

"I'd love to," Brody said. "But Melanie would have my hide. She's due the beginning of March and if I'm not here when the baby's born, there will be hell to pay."

"Maybe you can join the crew afterward," Stan suggested. "The boss seems to think we'll be there fifteen to eighteen months."

"Which is pretty much the first year and more of my son's life," Brody pointed out.

"It's a boy, huh?"

"Yeah," Brody confirmed, and she could hear the pride and pleasure in his voice. "The latest ultrasound confirmed it."

The conversation continued on that topic and Lauryn continued on her way to Kylie's room. But the whole time she was putting her daughter's clothes away, the workers' voices echoed in her head. *Watkinsville. Fifteen to eighteen months. Watkinsville…*

She dumped the dirty laundry from the bathroom hamper into the basket and had turned to head back downstairs, almost colliding with Brody when he stepped out of the master bedroom.

"Let me take that for you," he offered.

"Thanks," she said, relinquishing her hold on the basket, though the weight of it was insignificant compared to the heaviness in her heart.

"Do you like the new main floor laundry?" he asked, as they headed in that direction.

"I love it," she told him. "It's a relief not having to carry everything down to the basement and back up again."

"I imagine, with two little ones, you're doing a lot of laundry."

"Constantly," she agreed, marveling at the ease with which she was managing to make conversation despite the fact that her heart was breaking. "I hear you're going to have a little one soon, too."

The expectant father nodded. "Early March, if the baby comes on schedule."

"Babies come on their own schedules," she told him.

He grinned. "Yeah, I've already been warned."

As she followed Brody to the new laundry room, she realized that, with two exceptions, Ryder had left his mark in every single room of her house. In addition to the complete overhaul of the kitchen, his crew had patched and painted most of the other rooms, added new crown moldings and trim and updated the lighting. They'd refinished the fireplace and added built-in bookcases in the den, replaced all of the bathroom fixtures, vanities and tile. She had yet to see what they'd done in the master bedroom, but she didn't doubt that it would be equally fabulous. The only two rooms that hadn't been touched were Kylie's and Zachary's rooms. But there, Ryder had left his stamp on their hearts.

This house hadn't been her first choice when she and Rob were looking to buy, but she'd seen the potential in it and believed he would help with the necessary work to make it more distinctly their own. After her husband left, she'd hated the house and viewed every room as just another promise unfulfilled.

Ryder had given her back her home. When she looked around now, she loved everything about it because it felt as if it was truly hers. But not exclusively, because Ryder was everywhere. In every room, she saw not just the changes he'd made but the light of his smile and the sparkle in his eyes; she heard the echo of his voice and the sound of his laughter in the walls. It wasn't just her house—it was the house that Ryder built for her, and she really wished he could stay and share it with her and Kylie and Zachary. But that, she realized now, was a foolish wish.

She'd become so accustomed to having him around she hadn't let herself think about what would happen when the renovations were complete. Of course, he would move on to other projects—she'd always known that. But she hadn't anticipated that moving on would mean moving away.

And far more troubling to her than the realization that he was leaving was his complete silence on the subject. He'd told her about the Georgia project almost two months earlier, lamenting the delays and questioning whether the owners would ever get the necessary approvals to proceed with the work. But he hadn't mentioned it again since then.

The way Stan and Brody had been talking upstairs, the project was a go, with the team heading to Georgia early in the New Year. And Ryder hadn't said one word.

The only explanation she could imagine to explain his silence was that he'd never intended for their relationship to last beyond the completion of this project. When he was finished with her renovations, he would be finished with her, too.

She sorted through the laundry, tossing the darks into the washing machine and fighting back the tears that burned her eyes. After everything she'd been through in the past year, she wasn't going to fall apart over the end of a short-term relationship.

Except that she hadn't thought of it as a short-term relationship. Even in the beginning, when she'd tried to convince herself that she didn't want anything more than a casual fling, her heart had never believed it. And as the days had turned into weeks, she'd thought they were building something together. Or had she misread his signals?

But he was the one who'd convinced her to introduce him to her family at Thanksgiving. He was the one who'd told her that he loved her. And he'd made her fall all the way, head over heels in love with him in return. Even more damning, he'd made her children fall in love with him. Kylie and Zachary lit up whenever he walked into a room. They looked forward to seeing him every day—and they were going to be devastated when he was gone.

And once again she would be left behind to pick up the broken pieces of all of their hearts. It was her own fault. She'd known it was too soon, too risky. But her foolish heart had refused to be dissuaded.

And what was she supposed to do now? How could she continue to pretend that everything was okay when it was only a matter of time before he walked away from them?

The answer was simple—she couldn't. And since he hadn't told her about the Watkinsville project, she attempted to broach the subject herself.

"When do you think your crew is going to finish up here?" she asked Ryder later that night.

"If everything goes according to schedule, we should be done by the end of next week," he told her.

"And what are your plans after that?"

"After that, we'll take a few weeks off so everyone can enjoy the holidays with their families."

"Do you have any special plans?" she prompted.

He put his arms around her and brushed his lips against hers. "To spend as much time as possible with you."

Then he kissed her again until she forgot about pressing him for more details. Until she forgot about everything but how wonderful it felt to be in his arms.

* * *

She tried again the next morning, but his answers continued to be noncommittal and evasive. Even when she asked him point-blank about the Georgia restoration, he only said that Owen was working on it.

She gave up asking and decided just to enjoy the time they had together now and store up all the memories she could for the lonely days and nights after he was gone.

But apparently she wasn't as successful at hiding her true feelings as she thought. While Christmas shopping with her sisters, they decided to take a break and indulge in peppermint mochas.

"What's going on with you?" Jordyn asked her, when they'd settled at a table with their beverages. "Physically you're here, but your mind is obviously somewhere else."

"I'm guessing it's with Ryder," Tristyn teased.

"I'm sorry. I was thinking about Ryder," she admitted. "And the expiration date on our relationship."

Jordyn frowned. "What are you talking about?"

"He's packing up his tools and moving to Watkinsville in the New Year," she said miserably.

"Watkinsville, Georgia?" Tristyn asked.

She nodded.

"Why would he be going there?"

"For the next *Ryder to the Rescue* project."

"So he'll be gone a few weeks," her youngest sister said, unconcerned. "And then he'll be back."

But Lauryn shook her head. "It's a major restoration that will take months, maybe more than a year."

"Well, Watkinsville isn't that far," Jordyn pointed out.

"No," she agreed. "But he hasn't said anything to me about what's going to happen when he's gone. He hasn't even told me about the project."

"Then how do you know he's going?" Tristyn asked.

"I heard a couple of the guys talking about it, but Ryder

hasn't said a word. Doesn't that tell me everything I need to know?"

"I don't think it does," Jordyn denied.

"And I don't think you should jump to any conclusions without talking to him," Tristyn added.

"I've tried talking to him," she admitted. "And his answers to my questions are all deliberately vague."

"That doesn't sound like him."

"I didn't think so, either. And as incredible as the past two months have been with him, I have to accept that there's not going to be a storybook ending for us."

"We know you're wary of being hurt again," Tristyn said gently. "But I think, if you give him a chance, you'll discover that Ryder is your Prince Charming."

Lauryn shook her head. "It's long past time for me to stop believing in fairy tales."

"Just be careful not to close the book before the last page is written," Jordyn cautioned.

A few days later, when Lauryn found herself still mulling over her middle sister's cryptic remark, she decided that she was making too much of it. As the illustrator of AK Channing's stories, Jordyn lived in a world of science fiction and fantasy, but Lauryn had to face the realities of her current situation.

And then, one night early in December when she was tucking the kids into bed, Ryder slipped out of the house to get something from his truck.

Lauryn finished reading Kylie's bedtime story, then made her way back down the stairs just as Ryder was setting an enormous dollhouse down in the middle of the living room.

No, not a dollhouse, she realized. An absolutely breathtaking fairy-tale castle.

"Did you make this?" she asked, seriously amazed by the magnitude of the project.

He nodded. "It's for Kylie. For Christmas."

"Christmas is still three weeks away," she pointed out.

"I know, but I wanted to show it to you." He opened it up so that she could see the inside. "What do you think?"

"It's stunning," she told him, kneeling to more closely inspect the details.

"I didn't make the furniture and accessories," he admitted. "Those were beyond my skills—or at least my patience."

But every room was immaculately decorated and beautifully furnished. The windows had lace curtains, the floors had wool rugs and there were miniature portraits and paintings on the walls. The bedrooms had fancy beds with quilted covers, wardrobes and dressers; the nursery had a cradle, a change table and rocking chair; the bathroom had a toilet, a claw-foot tub and even an oval mirror above the pedestal sink. There were dishes in the kitchen cabinets, books on the shelves in the library and even a laundry room with a washer, dryer, iron and board.

"So who did the decorating?" she wondered.

"Monica Snyder—the show's interior designer. She was desperate for something to do while her leg is healing."

"This is amazing," she said.

"And check this out." He knelt beside her and touched a button beside the center door, illuminating all of the chandeliers and lamps—even the flames in the fireplace flickered.

"Kylie's going to love it," she told him. "Unfortunately, you've set the bar a little high for Santa now."

"What do you mean?"

"No other Christmas gift is ever going to top that."

"We'll see," he said vaguely.

"Don't you dare give her a puppy," she warned.

He chuckled. "I'm not going to give her a puppy—at least not this year."

Not this year. The implication being that there would be other years, other Christmases. But how could that be?

He was leaving in the New Year, and he still hadn't told her about his plans.

He tipped her chin up, forcing her to look at him. She swallowed the lump in her throat.

"That's the problem, isn't it?" he asked softly. "You don't want to think about future Christmases because you don't think I'm planning to stick around."

"I know you're going to Georgia after the holidays," she told him.

"And how do you know that?"

"I heard Brody and Stan talking about it," she admitted.

"They shouldn't have been discussing future projects that haven't been finalized."

"Fifteen to eighteen months in Watkinsville sounds pretty final to me."

"It's not quite a done deal," he told her. "We're still waiting for one last approval."

"What's holding things up?"

"I am."

Of all the responses he could have given to her question, Lauryn hadn't anticipated that one. "What? *Why?*"

"Because I wasn't going to say yes without talking to you first."

"I know how excited you are about this restoration," she told him. "I wouldn't ever ask you not to go."

He took her hands in his. "The question is—will you go with me?"

He wasn't planning to leave her; he wanted her to go to Georgia with him. And while that realization lessened the ache in her heart, it didn't change the reality of the situation. "I want to say yes," she admitted.

"Then say yes," he urged.

But she shook her head. "I can't walk away from my life for a whole year, maybe a year and a half, to be with you in Georgia."

"I'm not asking you to walk away from your life," he explained patiently. "I'm asking you to start a new life, a new family, with me."

Every beat of her heart was a yes, but her heart was often impulsive and foolish. She needed to think about this logically rather than emotionally. "I have responsibilities here," she reminded him. "The business—"

"Adam is more than capable of handling the business. That's why you hired him."

"And Kylie's going to start kindergarten next September."

"There are schools in Georgia," he pointed out. "In fact, there's an excellent primary school only a five-minute walk from the guesthouse on the property, where we could live while the renovations are happening."

"You've already looked at schools," she realized.

"I even have the registration forms."

"But...why?"

He squeezed her hands gently. "Because I know that you don't make any decisions without considering your children. Because I understand that you and Kylie and Zachary are a package deal. And because I want the whole package, Lauryn. Because I love you—all of you."

She had to swallow around the lump in her throat before she could reply. "I never wanted to fall in love again," she said softly, looking deep into his eyes. "But you didn't give me a choice. You barged into my life without invitation and started knocking down walls—" she smiled a little "—literally and metaphorically—and you made me see how much better my life could be with you in it. How much better my children's lives could be. And you made all of us fall in love with you. And I do love you, Ryder. With my whole heart," she finally admitted.

"Then say yes," he urged, releasing one of her hands to take a ring out of his pocket and offer it to her. "Not just to coming to Georgia, but making a life with me. Let me be your husband and Kylie and Zachary's stepfather. Let us be a family."

She was dazzled by his proposal even more than the diamond in his hand, but... "You said you weren't the forever-after type," she reminded him.

"Because I wasn't...until I met you."

"You also said love was a gamble."

"And I'm willing to go for broke," he told her. "Because I know that as long as you're by my side, I can't lose."

She saw the conviction in his eyes, felt it in her heart. They could make this work—they *would* make this work. "You have all the answers, don't you?"

"Not quite," he said. "I'm still waiting for yours."

She didn't make him wait any longer. "My answer is yes. With one minor amendment."

"Anything," he promised.

"I want you to be my husband," she told him. "But I'm not looking for a stepfather for my children. They need a real father. They deserve a full-time, forever-after kind of dad."

"Do you think I could be that kind of dad?" he asked, a little cautiously.

She lifted her free hand to his cheek. "You already are."

He slid the ring on her hand, and it was as perfect a fit for her finger as he was for her life. And then he kissed her, and it was a perfect kiss, too.

"I think my sister was right," she murmured.

"What was she right about?"

"I should never have tried to guess our ending—or given up hope that it would be a happy one."

"She was only partly right," he said. "This isn't an ending—it's our happy beginning."

Epilogue

On Christmas morning, Kylie awoke early, excited to discover what presents Santa had left for her and Zachary. 'Cept Mama had one very strict rule—no presents could be opened until everyone was awake. But that didn't mean she couldn't sneak downstairs and just *peek* at what was under the tree, did it?

She climbed out of bed and stuffed her feet into her slippers, then tiptoed to the stairs. She held tight on to the handrail as she made her way down. Some of the steps used to make a scary sound when she stepped on them. Mama said they groaned like an old man, but Ryder fixed that. Ryder fixed a lot of things that used to be broken—like the roof. Now even when it rained really, really hard, with thunder and lightning and everything, it didn't rain in her castle.

She was going to miss her castle when they went to… Watkin-something. She scrunched up her face and tried real hard but she couldn't 'member the name. But Mama showed it to her on a map, and it didn't look very far away. Her tummy felt a little funny when she thought about moving, but Mama said it wasn't forever. Just till Ryder fixed all the things that needed fixing in some old house there; then they would come back here.

She reached the last step and tiptoed into the living room. There were lots of presents wrapped in bright paper, but it was the castle in front of the tree that made her breath stop inside her.

She took another step closer and dropped to her knees

for a better look. She reached out, wanting to touch it, but snatched her hand back. She was only s'posed to peek, but now she really wanted to see what was inside.

She heard footsteps on the stairs and quickly backed away from the castle, climbing up onto the sofa so that she wouldn't get in trouble for peeking.

Ryder smiled at her from the doorway. "I thought I heard someone tiptoeing around down here."

"I twied to be quiet," Kylie whispered.

"Why did you try to be quiet?" he asked. "Don't you want to open your presents?"

She nodded. "But Mama said no pwesents till everyone is awake."

"Then we need to go back upstairs, stomping our feet the whole way, to wake them up, don't we?"

Kylie giggled. "Will Mama get mad?"

"Nah. Not on Christmas," he promised.

She slid off the edge of the sofa again but couldn't resist another peek at the presents under the tree.

"You're looking at that castle," he guessed.

She nodded. "Do you think it's for me?" she whispered the question.

"Let's find out," he said, taking her hand and guiding her closer. "Is your name on the tag?"

She couldn't print her name yet but she knew how to read it. She nodded as her finger pointed to each letter. "K-Y-L-I-E."

"That's right—it says 'To Kylie, From Santa.'"

She felt her mouth smile but she couldn't find any words to say.

He crouched down beside her. "Do you want to look inside?"

She nodded her head up and down.

So Ryder showed her the latch on the side, then helped her open it up. Her breath stopped again as the castle unfolded. She didn't know where to look—there was so much to see, so many rooms with lots of stuff inside.

"Did Santa do pretty good with this present then?" he asked, after she'd looked it all over.

"It's—" she need a second to 'member the word "—awesome."

He smiled. "The bestest present ever?"

She didn't have to think about the question long before she shook her head. "The bestest present ever is my new daddy."

His eyes were shiny when he hugged her. "I'm glad," he said. "Because your mom and you and Zachary are my bestest presents ever, too."

Kylie put her arms around his neck and kissed his scratchy cheek. "Can we wake Mama an' Zack now?" she asked him.

Ryder smiled. "Absolutely."

Then he took her hand and they stomped up the stairs together.

* * * * *

Single mom Andrea Montgomery only agreed to
look in on injured sheriff Marshall Bailey as a favor to
his sister, but when these lonely hearts are snowed in
together, there's no telling what Christmas wishes
might come true.

Turn the page for a sneak peek of
SNOWFALL ON HAVEN POINT
by New York Times *bestselling author*
RaeAnne Thayne,
available October 2016
wherever Harlequin books and ebooks are sold!

CHAPTER ONE

SHE REALLY NEEDED to learn how to say no once in a while.

Andrea Montgomery stood on the doorstep of the small, charming stone house just down the street from hers on Riverbend Road, her arms loaded with a tray of food that was cooling by the minute in the icy December wind blowing off the Hell's Fury River.

Her hands on the tray felt clammy and the flock of butterflies that seemed to have taken up permanent residence in her stomach jumped around maniacally. She didn't want to be here. Marshall Bailey, the man on the other side of that door, made her nervous under the best of circumstances.

This moment definitely did not fall into that category.

How could she turn down any request from Wynona Bailey, though? She owed Wynona whatever she wanted. The woman had taken a bullet for her, after all. If Wyn wanted her to march up and down the main drag in Haven Point wearing a tutu and combat boots, she would rush right out and try to find the perfect ensemble.

She would almost prefer that to Wyn's actual request but her friend had sounded desperate when she called earlier that day from Boise, where she was in graduate school to become a social worker.

"It's only for a week or so, until I can wrap things up here with my practicum and Mom and Uncle Mike make it back from their honeymoon," Wyn had said.

"It's not a problem at all," she had assured her. Apparently she was better at telling fibs than she thought because Wynona didn't even question her.

"Trust my brother to break his leg the one week that his mother and both of his sisters are completely unavailable to help him. I think he did it on purpose."

"Didn't you tell me he was struck by a hit-and-run driver?"

"Yes, but the timing couldn't be worse, with Katrina out of the country and Mom and Uncle Mike on their cruise until the end of the week. Marshall assures me he doesn't need help, but the man has a compound fracture, for crying out loud. He's not supposed to be weight-bearing at all. I would feel better the first few days he's home from the hospital if I knew that someone who lived close by could keep an eye on him."

Andie didn't want to be that someone. But how could she say no to Wynona?

It was a good thing her friend had been a police officer until recently. If Wynona had wanted a partner in crime, *Thelma & Louise* style, Andie wasn't sure she could have said no.

"Aren't you going to ring the doorbell, Mama?" Chloe asked, eyes apprehensive and her voice wavering a little. Her daughter was picking up her own nerves, Andie knew, with that weird radar kids had, but she had also become much more timid and anxious since the terrifying incident that summer when Wyn and Cade Emmett had rescued them all.

"I can do it," her four-year-old son, Will, offered. "My feet are *freezing* out here."

Her heart filled with love for both of her funny, sweet, wonderful children. Will was the spitting image of Jason while Chloe had his mouth and his eyes.

This would be their third Christmas without him and

she had to hope she could make it much better than the previous two.

She repositioned the tray and forced herself to focus on the matter at hand. "Sorry, I was thinking of something else."

She couldn't very well tell her children that she hadn't knocked yet because she was too busy thinking about how much she didn't want to be here.

"I told you that Sheriff Bailey has a broken leg and can't get around very well. He probably can't make it to the door easily and I don't want to make him get up. He should be expecting us. Wynona said she was calling him."

She transferred the tray to one arm just long enough to knock a couple of times loudly and twist the doorknob, which gave way easily. The door was blessedly unlocked.

"Sheriff Bailey? Hello? It's Andrea Montgomery."

"And Will and Chloe Montgomery," her son called helpfully, and Andie had to smile, despite the nerves jangling through her.

An instant later, she heard a crash, a thud and a muffled groan.

"Sheriff Bailey?"

"Not really...a good time."

She couldn't miss the pain in the voice of Wynona's older brother. It made her realize how ridiculous she was being. The man had been through a terrible ordeal in the last twenty-four hours and all she could think about was how much he intimidated her.

Nice, Andie. Feeling small and ashamed, she set the tray down on the nearest flat surface, a small table in the foyer still decorated in Wyn's quirky, fun style even though her brother had been living in the home since late August.

"Kids, wait right here for a moment," she said.

Chloe immediately planted herself on the floor by the door, her features taking on the fearful look she had worn too frequently since Rob Warren burst back into their lives so violently. Will, on the other hand, looked bored already. How had her children's roles reversed so abruptly? Chloe used to be the brave one, charging enthusiastically past any challenge, while Will had been the more tentative child.

"Do you need help?" Chloe asked tentatively.

"No. Stay here. I'll be right back."

She was sure the sound had come from the room where Wyn had spent most of her time when she lived here, a space that served as den, family room and TV viewing room in one. Her gaze immediately went to Marshall Bailey, trying to heft himself back up to the sofa from the floor.

"Oh, no!" she exclaimed. "What happened?"

"What do you think happened?" he growled. "You knocked on the door, so I tried to get up to answer and the damn crutches slipped out from under me."

"I'm so sorry. I only knocked to give you a little warning before we barged in. I didn't mean for you to get up."

He glowered. "Then you shouldn't have come over and knocked on the door."

She hated any conversation that came across as a confrontation. They always made her want to hide away in her room like she was a teenager again in her grandfather's house. It was completely immature of her, she knew. Grown-ups couldn't always walk away.

"Wyn asked me to check on you. Didn't she tell you?"

"I haven't talked to her since yesterday. My phone ran out of juice and I haven't had a chance to charge it."

By now, the county sheriff had pulled himself back onto the sofa and was trying to position pillows for his leg that sported a black orthopedic boot from his toes to just below his knee. His features contorted as he tried to reach the pillows but he quickly smoothed them out again. The man was obviously in pain and doing his best to conceal it.

She couldn't leave him to suffer, no matter how nervous his gruff demeanor made her.

She hurried forward and pulled the second pillow into place. "Is that how you wanted it?" she asked.

"For now."

She had a sudden memory of seeing the sheriff the night Rob Warren had broken into her home, assaulted her, held her at gunpoint and ended up in a shoot-out with the Haven Point police chief, Cade Emmett. He had burst into her home after the situation had been largely defused, to find Cade on the ground trying to revive a bleeding Wynona.

The stark fear on Marshall's face had haunted her, knowing that she might have unwittingly contributed to him losing another sibling after he had already lost his father and a younger brother in the line of duty.

Now Marshall's features were a shade or two paler and his eyes had the glassy, distant look of someone in a great deal of pain.

"How long have you been out of the hospital?"

He shrugged. "A couple hours. Give or take."

"And you're here by yourself?" she exclaimed. "I thought you were supposed to be home earlier this morning and someone was going to stay with you for the first few hours. Wynona told me that was the plan."

"One of my deputies drove me home from the hospital but I told him Chief Emmett would probably keep an eye on me."

The police chief lived across the street from Andie and just down the street from Marshall, which boded well for crime prevention in the neighborhood. Having the sheriff *and* the police chief on the same street should be any sane burglar's worst nightmare—especially *this* particular sheriff and police chief.

"And has he been by?"

"Uh, no. I didn't ask him to." Marshall's eyes looked

unnaturally blue in his pain-tight features. "Did my sister send you to babysit me?"

"Babysit, no. She only asked me to periodically check on you. I also brought dinner for the next few nights."

"Also unnecessary. If I get hungry, I'll call Serrano's for a pizza later."

She gave him a bland look. "Would a pizza delivery driver know to come pick you up off the floor?"

"You didn't pick me up," he muttered. "You just moved a few pillows around."

He must find this completely intolerable, being dependent on others for the smallest thing. In her limited experience, most men made difficult patients. Tough, take-charge guys like Marshall Bailey probably hated every minute of it.

Sympathy and compassion had begun to replace some of her nervousness. She would probably never truly like the man—he was so big, so masculine, a cop through and through—but she could certainly empathize with what he was going through. For now, he was a victim and she certainly knew what that felt like.

"I brought dinner, so you might as well eat it," she said. "You can order pizza tomorrow if you want. It's not much, just beef stew and homemade rolls, with caramel apple pie for dessert."

"Not much?" he said, eyebrow raised. A low rumble sounded in the room just then and it took her a moment to realize it was coming from his stomach.

"You don't have to eat it, but if you'd like some, I can bring it in here."

He opened his mouth but before he could answer, she heard a voice from the doorway.

"What happened to you?" Will asked, gazing at Marshall's assorted scrapes, bruises and bandages with wide-eyed fascination.

"Will, I thought I told you to wait for me by the door."

"I know, but you were taking *forever*." He walked into the room a little farther, not at all intimidated by the battered, dangerous-looking man it contained. "Hi. My name is Will. What's yours?"

The sheriff gazed at her son. If anything, his features became even more remote, but he might have simply been in pain.

"This is Sheriff Bailey," Andie said, when Marshall didn't answer for a beat too long. "He's Wynona's brother."

Will beamed at him as if Marshall was his new best friend. "Wynona is nice and she has a nice dog whose name is Young Pete, only Wynona said he's not young anymore."

"Yeah, I know Young Pete," Marshall said after another pause. "He's been in our family for a long time. He was our dad's dog first."

Andie gave him a careful look. From Wyn, she knew their father had been shot in the line of duty several years earlier and had suffered a severe brain injury that left him physically and cognitively impaired. John Bailey had died the previous winter from pneumonia, after spending his last years at a Shelter Springs care center.

Though she had never met the man, her heart ached to think of all the Baileys had suffered.

"Why is his name Young Pete?" Will asked. "I think that's silly. He should be just Pete."

"Couldn't agree more, but you'll have to take that up with my sister."

Will accepted that with equanimity. He took another step closer and scrutinized the sheriff. "How did you get so hurt? Were you in a fight with some bad guys? Did you shoot them? A bad guy came to our house once and Chief Emmett shot him."

Andie stepped in quickly. She was never sure how much Will understood about what happened that summer. "Will, I need your help fixing a tray with dinner for the sheriff."

"I want to hear about the bad guys, though."

"There were no bad guys. I was hit by a car," Marshall said abruptly.

"You're big! Don't you know you're supposed to look both ways and hold someone's hand?"

Marshall Bailey's expression barely twitched. "I guess nobody happened to be around at the time."

Torn between amusement and mortification, Andie grabbed her son's hand. "Come on, Will," she said, her tone insistent. "I need your help."

Her put-upon son sighed. "Okay."

He let her hold his hand as they went back to the entry, where Chloe still sat on the floor, watching the hallway with anxious eyes.

"I told Will not to go in when you told us to wait here but he wouldn't listen to me," Chloe said fretfully.

"You should see the police guy," Will said with relish. "He has blood on him and everything."

Andie hadn't seen any blood but maybe Will was more observant than she. Or maybe he had just become good at trying to get a rise out of his sister.

"Ew. Gross," Chloe exclaimed, looking at the doorway with an expression that contained equal parts revulsion and fascination.

"He is Wyn's brother and knows Young Pete, too," Will informed her.

Easily distracted, as most six-year-old girls could be, Chloe sighed. "I miss Young Pete. I wonder if he and Sadie will be friends?"

"Why wouldn't they be?" Will asked.

"Okay, kids, we can talk about Sadie and Young Pete another time. Right now, we need to get dinner for Wynona's brother."

"I need to use the bathroom," Will informed her. He had

that urgent look he sometimes wore when he had pushed things past the limit.

"There's a bathroom just down the hall, second door down. See?"

"Okay."

He raced for it—she hoped in time.

"We'll be in the kitchen," she told him, then carried the food to the bright and spacious room with its stainless appliances and white cabinets.

"See if you can find a small plate for the pie while I dish up the stew," she instructed Chloe.

"Okay," her daughter said.

The nervous note in her voice broke Andie's heart, especially when she thought of the bold child who used to run out to confront the world.

"Do I have to carry it out there?" Chloe asked.

"Not if you don't want to, honey. You can wait right here in the kitchen or in the entryway, if you want."

While Chloe perched on one of the kitchen stools and watched, Andie prepared a tray for him, trying to make it as tempting as possible. She had a feeling his appetite wouldn't be back to normal for a few days because of the pain and the aftereffects of anesthesia but at least the fault wouldn't lie in her presentation.

It didn't take long, but it still gave her time to make note of the few changes in the kitchen. In the few months Wynona had been gone, Marshall Bailey had left his mark. The kitchen was clean but not sparkling, and where Wyn had kept a cheery bowl of fruit on the counter, a pair of handcuffs and a stack of mail cluttered the space. Young Pete's food and water bowls were presumably in Boise with Young Pete.

As she looked at the space on the floor where they usually rested, she suddenly remembered dogs weren't the only creatures who needed beverages.

"I forgot to fill Sheriff Bailey's water bottle," she said to Chloe. "Could you do that for me?"

Chloe hopped down from her stool and picked up the water bottle. With her bottom lip pressed firmly between her teeth, she filled the water bottle with ice and water from the refrigerator before screwing the lid back on and held it out for Andie.

"Thanks, honey. Oh, the tray's pretty full and I don't have a free hand. I guess I'll have to make another trip for it."

As she had hoped, Chloe glanced at the tray and then at the doorway with trepidation on her features that eventually shifted to resolve.

"I guess I can maybe carry it for you," she whispered.

Andie smiled and rubbed a hand over her hair, heart bursting with pride at this brave little girl. "Thank you, Chloe. You're always such a big help to me."

Chloe mustered a smile, though it didn't stick. "You'll be right there?"

"The whole time. Where do you suppose that brother of yours is?"

She suspected the answer, even before she and Chloe walked back to the den and she heard Will chattering.

"And I want a new Lego set and a sled and some real walkie-talkies like my friend Ty has. He has his own pony and I want one of those, too, only my mama says I can't have one because we don't have a place for him to run. Ty lives on a ranch and we only have a little backyard and we don't have a barn or any hay for him to eat. That's what horses eat—did you know that?"

Rats. Had she actually been stupid enough to fall for that "I have to go to the bathroom" gag? She should have known better. Will had probably raced right back in here the moment her back was turned.

"I did know that. And oats and barley, too," Sheriff Bailey said. His voice, several octaves below Will's, rippled down her spine. Did he sound annoyed? She couldn't tell. Mostly, his voice sounded remote.

"We have oatmeal at our house and my mom puts barley in soup sometimes, so why couldn't we have a pony?"

She should probably rescue the man. He just had one leg broken by a hit-and-run driver. He didn't need the other one talked off by an almost-five-year-old. She moved into the room just in time to catch the tail end of the discussion.

"A pony is a pretty big responsibility," Marshall said.

"So is a dog and a cat and we have one of each, a dog named Sadie and a cat named Mrs. Finnegan," Will pointed out.

"But a pony is a lot more work than a dog *or* a cat. Anyway, how would one fit on Santa's sleigh?"

Judging by his peal of laughter, Will apparently thought that was hilarious.

"He couldn't! You're silly."

She had to wonder if anyone had ever called the serious sheriff *silly* before. She winced and carried the tray inside the room, judging it was past time to step in.

"Here you go. Dinner. Again, don't get your hopes up. I'm an adequate cook but that's about it."

She set the food down on the end table next to the sofa and found a folded wooden TV tray she didn't remember from her frequent visits to the house when Wynona lived here. She set up the TV tray and transferred the food to it, then gestured for Chloe to bring the water bottle. Her daughter hurried over without meeting his gaze, set the bottle on the tray, then rushed back to the safety of the kitchen as soon as she could.

Marshall looked at the tray, then at her, leaving her feeling as if *she* were the silly one.

"Thanks. It looks good. I appreciate your kindness," he said stiffly, as if the words were dragged out of him.

He had to know any kindness on her part was out of obligation toward Wynona. The thought made her feel rather guilty. He was her neighbor and she should be more enthusiastic about helping him, whether he made her nervous or not.

"Where is your cell phone?" she asked. "You need some way to contact the outside world."

"Why?"

She frowned. "Because people are concerned about you! You just got out of the hospital a few hours ago. You need pain medicine at regular intervals and you're probably supposed to have ice on that leg or something."

"I'm fine, as long as I can get to the bathroom and the kitchen and I have the remote close at hand."

Such a typical man. She huffed out a breath. "At least think of the people who care about you. Wyn is out of her head with worry, especially since your mother and Katrina aren't in town."

"Why do you think I didn't charge my phone?" he muttered.

She crossed her arms across her chest. She didn't like confrontation or big, dangerous men any more than her daughter did, but Wynona had asked her to watch out for him and she took the charge seriously.

"You're being obstinate. What if you trip over your crutches and hit your head, only this time somebody isn't at the door to make sure you can get up again?"

"That's not going to happen."

"You don't know that. Where is your phone, Sheriff?"

He glowered at her but seemed to accept the inevitable. "Fine," he said with a sigh. "It should be in the pocket of my jacket, which is in the bag they sent home with me from the hospital. I think my deputy said he left it in the bedroom. First door on the left."

The deputy should have made sure his boss had some

way to contact the outside world, but she had a feeling it was probably a big enough chore getting Sheriff Bailey home from the hospital without him trying to drive himself and she decided to give the poor guy some slack.

"I'm going to assume the charger is in there, too."

"Yeah. By the bed."

She walked down the hall to the room that had once been Wyn's bedroom. The bedroom still held traces of Wynona in the solid Mission furniture set but Sheriff Bailey had stamped his own personality on it in the last three months. A Stetson hung on one of the bedposts, and instead of mounds of pillows and the beautiful log cabin quilt Wyn's aunts had made her, a no-frills but soft-looking navy duvet covered the bed, made neatly as he had probably left it the morning before. A pile of books waited on the bedside table and a pair of battered cowboy boots stood toe-out next to the closet.

The room smelled masculine and entirely too sexy for her peace of mind, of sage-covered mountains with an undertone of leather and spice.

Except for that brief moment when she had helped him back to the sofa, she had never been close enough to Marshall to see if that scent clung to his skin. The idea made her shiver a little before she managed to rein in the wholly inappropriate reaction.

She found the plastic hospital bag on the wide armchair near the windows, overlooking the snow-covered pines along the river. Feeling strangely guilty at invading the man's privacy, she opened it. At the top of the pile that appeared to contain mostly clothing, she found another large clear bag with a pair of ripped jeans inside covered in a dried dark substance she realized was blood.

Marshall Bailey's blood.

The stark reminder of his close call sent a tremor through her. He could have been killed if that hit-and-run driver had struck him at a slightly higher rate of speed. The Baileys likely wouldn't have recovered, especially since Wyn's twin brother, Wyatt, had been struck and killed by an out-of-control vehicle while helping a stranded motorist during a winter storm.

The jeans weren't ruined beyond repair. Maybe she could spray stain remover on them and try to mend the rips and tears.

Further searching through the bag finally unearthed the telephone. She found the charger next to the bed and carried the phone, charger and bag containing the Levi's back to the sheriff.

While she was gone from the room, he had pulled the tray close and was working on the dinner roll in a desultory way.

She plugged the charger into the same outlet as the lamp next to the sofa and inserted the other end into his phone. "Here you are. I'll let you turn it on. Now you'll have no excuse not to talk to your family when they call."

"Thanks. I guess."

Andie held out the bag containing the jeans. "Do you mind if I take these? I'd like to see if I can get the stains out and do a little repair work."

"It's not worth the effort. I don't even know why they sent them home. The paramedics had to cut them away to get to my leg."

"You never know. I might be able to fix them."

He shrugged, his eyes wearing that distant look again. He was in pain, she realized, and trying very hard not to show it.

"If you power on your phone and unlock it, I can put my cell number in there so you can reach me in an emergency."

"I won't—" he started to say but the sentence ended with a sigh as he reached for the phone.

As soon as he turned it on, the phone gave a cacophony

of beeps, alerting him to missed texts and messages, but he paid them no attention.

"What's your number?"

She gave it to him and in turn entered his into her own phone.

"Please don't be stubborn. If you need help, call me. I'm just a few houses away and can be here in under two minutes—and that's even if I have to take time to put on boots and a winter coat."

He likely wouldn't call and both of them knew it.

"Are we almost done?" Will asked from the doorway, clearly tired of having only his sister to talk to in the other room.

"In a moment," she said, then turned back to Marshall. "Do you know Herm and Louise Jacobs, next door?"

Oddly, he gaped at her for a long, drawn-out moment. "Why do you ask?" His voice was tight with suspicion.

"If I'm not around and you need help for some reason, they or their grandson Christopher can be here even faster. I'll put their number in your phone, too, just in case."

"I doubt I'll need it, but...thanks."

"Christopher has a skateboard, a big one," Will offered gleefully. "He rides it without even a helmet!"

Her son had a bad case of hero worship when it came to the Jacobses' troubled grandson, who had come to live with Herm and Louise shortly after Andie and her children arrived in Haven Point. It worried her a little to see how fascinated Will was with the clearly rebellious teenager, but so far Christopher had been patient and even kind to her son.

"That's not very safe, is it?" the sheriff said gruffly. "You should always wear a helmet when you're riding a bike or skateboard to protect your head."

"I don't even *have* a skateboard," Will said.

"If you get one," Marshall answered. This time she couldn't miss the clear strain in his voice. The man was at the end of his endurance and probably wanted nothing more than to be alone with his pain.

"We really do need to leave," Andie said quickly. "Is there anything else I can do to help you before we leave?"

He shook his head, then winced a little as if the motion hurt. "You've done more than enough already."

"Try to get some rest, if you can. I'll check in with you tomorrow and also bring something for your lunch."

He didn't exactly look overjoyed at the prospect. "I don't suppose I can say anything to persuade you otherwise, can I?"

"You're a wise man, Sheriff Bailey."

Will giggled. "Where's your gold and Frankenstein?"

Marshall blinked, obviously as baffled as she was, which only made Will giggle more.

"Like in the Baby Jesus story, you know. The wise men brought the gold, Frankenstein and mirth."

She did her best to hide a smile. This year Will had become fascinated with the small carved Nativity set she bought at a thrift store the first year she moved out of her grandfather's cheerless house.

"Oh. Frankincense and myrrh. They were perfumes and oils, I think. When I said Sheriff Bailey was a wise man, I just meant he was smart."

She was a little biased, yes, but she couldn't believe even the most hardened of hearts wouldn't find her son adorable. The sheriff only studied them both with that dour expression.

He was in pain, she reminded herself. If she were in his position, she wouldn't find a four-year-old's chatter amusing, either.

"We'll see you tomorrow," she said again. "Call me, even if it's the middle of the night."

"I will," he said, which she knew was a blatant fib. He would never call her.

She had done all she could, short of moving into his house—kids, pets and all.

She gathered the children part of that equation and ushered them out of the house. Darkness came early this close to the winter solstice but the Jacobs family's Christmas lights next door gleamed through the snow.

In the short time she'd been inside his house, Andie had forgotten most of her nervousness around Marshall. Perhaps it was his injury that made him feel a little less threatening to her—though she had a feeling that even if he'd suffered *two* broken legs in that accident, the sheriff of Lake Haven County would never be anything less than dangerous.

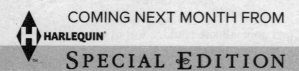
#2509 A CHILD UNDER HIS TREE
Return to the Double C • by Allison Leigh
Kelly Rasmussen and Caleb Buchanan were high school sweethearts until life got in the way. Now they're both back in Weaver and want a second chance, but everything is made more complicated by the five-year-old little boy with his secret father's eyes.

#2510 THE MAVERICK'S HOLIDAY SURPRISE
Montana Mavericks: The Baby Bonanza • by Karen Rose Smith
Trust-fund cowboy Hudson Jones wants Bella Stockton, but day-care babies and a secret stand in their way. Can Hudson help Bella overcome her intimacy fears—and can Bella convince the roaming cowboy that home for the holidays is the best place to be?

#2511 THE RANCHER'S EXPECTANT CHRISTMAS
Wed in the West • by Karen Templeton
When jilted—and hugely pregnant—Deanna Blake returns to Whispering Pines, New Mexico, for her father's funeral, single dad Josh Talbot sees everything he wants in a partner in the grown-up version of his old friend. But how can this uncomplicated country boy heal the city girl's broken heart?

#2512 CALLIE'S CHRISTMAS WISH
Three Coins in the Fountain • by Merline Lovelace
Callie Langston is *not* boring! And to prove it, she's going to Rome to work as a counselor to female refugees over Christmas. Security expert Joe Russo learned the hard way how cruel the world can be when his fiancé was murdered, and he plans on making sure Callie is protected—always. Even if that means he has to follow her halfway around the globe. But can Callie's thirst for adventure and Joe's protective instincts coexist long enough for her Christmas wish to come true?

#2513 THANKFUL FOR YOU
The Brands of Montana • by Joanna Sims
Dallas Dalton wants to mess up city-boy lawyer Nick Brand's perfectly controlled exterior from the moment they meet. Nick can't explain why he's drawn to the wild-child cowgirl, he just knows he is. But they come from completely different worlds, and it might just take a Thanksgiving miracle to prove to them they have more in common than they think.

#2514 THE COWBOY'S BIG FAMILY TREE
Hurley's Homestyle Kitchen • by Meg Maxwell
Christmas is coming and rancher Logan Grainger is struggling with the news that another man is his biological father. He recently became guardian to his orphaned nephews and learned that his new nine-year-old stepsister is being fostered by his old flame Clementine Hurley. She wants them to be a family, but can Logan move past the lies to bring them all together under a Christmas tree?

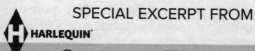
"Why do you care, Caleb?"

He was silent for so long she wasn't sure he was going to answer. And since he wasn't, she pushed away from the brick. "I need to get back to Tyler."

"I've always cared."

His words washed over her. Instead of feeling like a balmy wave, though, it felt like being rolled against abrasive sand. "Right." She stepped around him.

"Dammit." His hand shot out and he grabbed her arm.

She tried to shaking him off. "Let go."

"You asked and I'm telling you. So now you're going to walk away?" He let her go. "I swear, you're as stubborn as your mother."

She flinched.

He swore again. Thrust his fingers through his dark hair. "I didn't mean that."

Why not? She adored her son. Didn't regret his existence for one single second. In that, she was very different from her mother. But that didn't mean she wasn't Georgette Rasmussen's daughter with all the rest that that implied.

"I have to go." She tried stepping around his big body again.

"I'm sorry that I hurt you. I was always sorry, Kelly. Always."

She looked up at him. "But you did it anyway."

"And you're going to hate me forever because of it? It was nearly ten years ago!"

When he'd dumped her for another girl.

And only six years when she'd impetuously, angrily put her mouth on his and set in motion a situation she still couldn't change.

Which was worse?

His actions or hers?

Her eyes suddenly burned. Because she was pretty sure keeping the existence of his own son from him outweighed him falling in love with someone far better suited to him than simple little Kelly Rasmussen.

He made a rough sound of impatience. "If you're gonna hate me anyway—"

She barely had a chance to frown before his mouth hit hers.

Don't miss
A CHILD UNDER HIS TREE by Allison Leigh,
available November 2016 wherever
Harlequin® Special Edition books and ebooks are sold.

www.Harlequin.com

HSEEXP1016R

NEW YORK TIMES BESTSELLING AUTHOR

RaeAnne Thayne

SNOWFALL ON HAVEN POINT

A HAVEN POINT NOVEL

$7.99 U.S./$9.99 CAN.

EXCLUSIVE
Limited Time Offer

$1.⁰⁰ OFF

New York Times bestselling author

RaeAnne Thayne

There's no place like Haven Point for the holidays, where the snow conspires to bring two wary hearts together for a Christmas to remember.

SNOWFALL ON HAVEN POINT

Available September 27, 2016.
Pick up your copy today!

HQN™

- ✂

$1.⁰⁰ OFF
the purchase price of SNOWFALL ON HAVEN POINT by RaeAnne Thayne.

Offer valid from September 27, 2016, to October 31, 2016.
Redeemable at participating retail outlets. Not redeemable at Barnes & Noble.
Limit one coupon per purchase. Valid in the U.S.A. and Canada only.

52613933

5 65373 00076 2 (8100)0 12185

® and ™ are trademarks owned and used by the trademark owner and/or its licensee.

© 2016 Harlequin Enterprises Limited

PHCOUPRAT1016

THE WORLD IS BETTER WITH

Romance

4276

Harlequin has everything from contemporary, passionate and heartwarming to suspenseful and inspirational stories.

Whatever your mood, we have a romance just for you!

Connect with us to find your next great read, special offers and more.

f /HarlequinBooks

🐦 @HarlequinBooks

www.HarlequinBlog.com

www.Harlequin.com/Newsletters

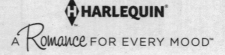

HARLEQUIN®

A *Romance* FOR EVERY MOOD™

www.Harlequin.com